Where There Is Life There Is Always Hope

Where There Is Life There Is Always Hope

A SEQUEL TO

It's a Wonderful Life

BY

Neil Mitchell

Printed in the United States of America

ISBN 979-8-89114-050-9 (sc)
ISBN 979-8-89114-051-6 (e)

Library of Congress Preassigned Control Number: 2023924531

2025.10.10

MainSpring Books
5901 W. Century Blvd
Suite 750
Los Angeles, CA, US, 90045

www.mainspringbooks.com

OTHER BOOKS BY NEIL MITCHELL

FICTION

A Stateside Tour of Duty

Small Silver Coins: A Tale of the American West

A Skeleton in the Closet:
The History of the Laslow Family

SEMI BIOGRAPHICAL,
BASED ON ACTUAL EVENTS

Where is the Glory:
A Saga of Tragedy and Triumph

NONFICTION

The Forgotten Years:
The Beginnings of Collegiate Football in Utah

The Great College Football Playoff Hoax

Preface

Few stories are as loved as the 1946 movie *It's A Wonderful Life*. The fictional David and Goliath story of the small Bailey Building and Loan business surviving constant challenges from their nemesis Henry Potter and ever-present economic problems inspires for all time. It reminds us that all people are interconnected. In the words of Poet John Donne, "No man is an island unto himself."

As the copyright on that beautiful story has been allowed to lapse into the public domain, I have taken the liberty of continuing the story into the decades of the mid- to late twentieth century.

As you read the story, you may notice that, with few exceptions, I do not describe the characters. This fact results from the Bailey family members fixed being in everyone's mind, as a result of the Oscar-nominated movie. Jack Curtis, the nephew of Henry Potter, is obviously white, but the reader may imagine the many other characters as any race they may desire.

In the twenty-first century, race is becoming irrelevant, so unless race is a meaningful part of the story (for example, Jack striving to get the wedding reception of Rod Burkhart and Zuzu held in his elite country club), the race of other individuals is never mentioned. Therefore, the reader may mentally picture company officials, townspeople, and other characters in any way they wish as a part of the American human panorama.

This story begins fifteen years after the movie ends, as a struggling rancher in Texas has an incredible financial windfall come into his life upon the death of his uncle, Henry Potter.

I hope readers enjoy this story as much as I enjoyed writing it. I also pray I have done justice to the original classic, which teaches us all that where ever there is life, there is always hope.

Neil Mitchell

Chapter One

As Jack Curtis drove his 1952 Ford pickup up the driveway by the house, he stopped to think. 1960 had not been a good year. A tornado had destroyed his barn the previous June and cattle prices were down. In addition, his only close relative, his stepbrother Dewey had passed away from a stroke in May.

Dewey's wife, April, had asked Jack for help with her husband's funeral. She then ordered an expensive service and stuck Jack with the bill. Dewey had been unable to work due to being a 1950s polio victim and April saw her brother-in-law as a wealthy rancher. As a result, she constantly imposed upon Jack and his family. Now, thirty days later, the nine-hundred-dollar funeral expense was added to the other bills he had to contend with.

In town, he had found the economic recession that began two years before was still plaguing the San Angelo area in contrast to the optimistic news relayed over the radio. Rising costs for feed and other expenses were continuing to be a problem. Sitting in his car, he said, "Just another typical Monday." Then with a smile he thought: *At least we're healthy. I never had horrible health like Dewey and suffered as he did.* Before getting out of the car he paused, and with a smile he considered another thing. *And I'm not married to someone like April. That witch has always wished her last name was Jones. At least Dewey is finally rid of her. Unfortunately, the poor guy had to die to do it.*

As he approached the front door, his wife Carole met him with a kiss. "It's good to see you smiling," she said. "That hasn't happened for several days."

"Honey, I was just thinking about my late step-brother. Compared to him, I have nothing to be unhappy about. Everyone in the family is healthy and you are nothing like that worthless, nagging, complaining woman he was married to. I'm lucky to be married to you."

"Well, it's about time you realized that," she proudly said. She then changed the subject. "Uh, some lawyer from New York called while you were gone. He says it's extremely important that you call him as soon as you got home. He said his name was Fred Rosenburg. Here's the number. He was insistent you call at once."

"I don't know anybody in New York. And this will be a long-distance call. Those aren't cheap." Jack complained.

"Well, he said it was urgent. Just make the call, honey. See what he wants."

"Fine," he said sarcastically. "I guess a little more bad news can't hurt that much."

He picked up the receiver from the base of the phone and reluctantly dialed a zero with his right index finger.

After a few seconds he heard, "Operator."

"Yes, ma'am. I need to place a long-distance call to New York." He then read the number.

"One moment, sir," the operator replied.

There were a few seconds before the phone rang on the other end. A secretary answered. "Hoffman, Abrams, and Rosenberg. How may I direct your call?"

"This is Jack Curtis from Wall, Texas. I was told I needed to speak to Mr. Rosenberg."

"Yes, Mr. Curtis, I'll buzz his office. He is expecting your call," the woman replied.

A few seconds later the attorney answered. "This is Fred Rosenberg."

"Jack Curtis here, sir. My wife said you had an urgent need to speak to me."

"Yes, Mr. Curtis, I regret to inform you that your uncle, Henry Potter, passed away yesterday morning, and according to his will, you are his only living relative and heir."

"Wow!" he sighed. "I never met Uncle Henry, and my mother rarely mentioned him. But I still need to order some flowers."

"Actually, sir, we would appreciate more than that. First, we need to assure the employees that Potter Industries will continue to function smoothly."

"Employees?" Jack said quizzically.

"Yes, Mr. Curtis, at the close of business Friday, the Henry Potter Trust was worth over sixty million dollars, and the company itself is worth thirty-one million. We are anxious to assure everyone there will be no crisis in a leadership change," Rosenberg explained.

Jack coughed and sputtered. "Excuse me, sir. I think we have a problem with the phone line. Did I hear you say sixty million dollars?"

Her cup of coffee almost slipped from Carole's fingers as she listened. She held on to the kitchen counter, steadying herself.

"Sixty million and change, sir," Rosenberg replied. "As your uncle's funeral is currently scheduled for Wednesday, we would appreciate you meeting with us before that to ensure the change in corporate leadership runs as smoothly as possible."

"It will take me at least three days to drive to New York," Jack said as he continued to consider what he was hearing.

"No need to drive, Mr. Curtis. We can have the corporate airplane there in less than six hours."

"I need to ensure my ranch is properly looked after and we need to pack. I want my wife to be there, too," Jack replied.

"I understand. How much time do you need?" the lawyer asked.

Looking at Carole, who still looked stunned, he asked while covering the phone with the palm of his hand, "Honey, how long will it take to pack for a trip to New York? They're sending the company plane."

"Three hours?" she replied in a questioning manner.

"Mr. Rosenberg," Jack replied confidently, "make it six hours so I can make sure my ranch is looked after while I'm gone."

"Excellent, I will call you the second our pilot has an ETA for his landing at the San Angelo airport." Then the lawyer added. "Do you have any further questions?"

With a smile, Jack said, "Not at this time, sir. But I look forward to meeting with you in New York." Then as he hung up the phone, his calm demeanor turned to near panic as he said, "Hurry and pack, I need to find someone to take care of the place while we're gone."

Carole, still totally confused, replied, "How long do I need to pack for?"

He thought for a second. "Four days. If we need more than that, we'll buy some new clothes there."

"Are you sure about that, honey?"

"Carole, according to the man I just talked too, I've inherited sixty million dollars. I'm sure we can afford another change of clothes if we need them. But, right now, I need to get some help with the ranch."

Before going to the bedroom to start packing, his wife asked, "Who died?"

"My Uncle, Henry Potter. Mother rarely mentioned him, and when she did, she never had anything good to say about him. I had no idea he was rich." Then, after another thought, he added, "Hurry and start packing. We can talk about it later. We don't have much time."

"What about the kids, honey?" Carole asked. "I won't leave them with April. I don't trust her."

Jack thought for a second. "We'll take them with us. Pack their clothes as well."

"Are you sure that's a good idea? They might not like that," Carole asked.

"Honey," he smiled, "apparently, I own the company. What in the world can they say? Now get your gorgeous butt moving and pack. Remember, we're short on time." With that he dialed another number as Carole left the room.

Chapter Two

Jack called Tom Barnes, who had worked part time for him the past four years. "Tom, I have a favor to ask."

"No problem. What can I do for you?" was the reply.

"I just found out that my uncle kicked the bucket in New York and I need to go get him planted. I need you to look after my ranch while I'm gone. It will take more hours than you normally put in, but I'll make it worth your while when I return."

"No problem, boss, and I'm sorry to hear of your loss. I'll take care of everything, so you don't have to worry."

"Thanks, Tom. I appreciate it."

"You're welcome and I hope things go well in New York."

After the call, Jack went to the bedroom where Carole was packing a suitcase. "Sweetheart, let's not mention money to the kids or anyone else. If April hears about the possibility of us coming into money, she will be more unbearable than she is now. I'm tired of her using us as her personal bank."

"I understand," she said. "The less said, the better. We are just going to New York for a funeral."

"That's right," her husband said with a smile. "We are only going there to pay our respects to Uncle Henry."

Four-year-old Liz, playing in the backyard was called in and ordered to take a bath. She was not happy.

"I took one yesterday," she complained.

"Sweetie," her mother said, "we must take a trip, and you need look your best."

Jack contacted their mail carrier and asked that no mail be delivered until he let them know they had returned. Then six-year-old David arrived from school. Like his sister, his mother told him that he needed to bathe.

Once the children were washed off, Carole told them to dress like they were going to church.

"Why, Mom?" David protested.

"Because we will fly on an airplane and you always dress up when you fly on a plane."

Suddenly the young boy stopped protesting. Then, with wide eyes, he exclaimed: "Wow! We get to fly on an airplane. When do we do that?"

"In a few hours," Carole replied. "We need to go to New York for the funeral of Daddy's uncle."

Things were hectic as they made sure they had everything necessary for the trip and tied up any loose ends. Shortly, Carole had three suitcases stuffed full of clothes and toiletries and they loaded the suitcases into their 1949 Mercury Coupe. As they did, Carole smiled and asked, "Honey, do you think we can buy a newer car now that hopefully we have a little more money? I know you're cheap but we need a new car."

Jack smiled. "I'm not cheap, sweetheart, I'm thrifty. But to make you happy, as soon as we return, I think we'll buy *two* new cars. One for each of us. But first, we must get to New York and learn more about what I'm inheriting."

About four hours later, they received a call from an employee of Potter Industries informing them that the plane would arrive at general aviation of the San Angelo airport at 8:03 P.M. That was two hours away.

"Carole," Jack said, "are you sure you have everything?"

"I hope so," she replied. "Do you think I look okay?"

Her husband laughed. "Sweetheart, you look like you're going to the Cattlemen's Association Christmas Ball. You look great." Then he asked her, "Should I wear a fedora or my Stetson for work?"

"Wear the fedora. It's a little more formal."

"But, honey, we're from Texas. Those folks will be expecting me to wear a cowboy-type hat," he suggested.

"I think you should avoid stereotypes and dress like the natives in New York," she said with a smile.

"Well, okay. You do keep me color-coordinated and dressed well. I'll accept the suggestion."

"I'm hungry!" David complained.

"Oh, my gosh! I forgot all about dinner," Carole apologized. "I was so busy packing I didn't even think about it."

"That's okay, sweetheart," Jack replied. "We will stop at a café. There's no reason to mess up the kitchen. Everyone take a look around and make sure we have everything."

"What about Mr. Giraffe?" four-year-old Liz asked.

While most children slept with a teddy bear, the stuffed animal Liz needed to sleep with each night was Mr. Giraffe. Knowing that forgetting him would be a disaster, Jack ran to Liz's bedroom and retrieved her favorite toy. He handed it to his daughter.

"Mr. Giraffe!" she squealed as she hugged the plush toy.

"Well, let's get out of here and head for the airport," Jack directed.

"I'm hungry!" little David exclaimed again.

"We'll get you some food on the way, champ," his father said. With that, they got into the eleven-year-old car and departed.

After stopping for something to eat at a diner on the outskirts of San Angelo, they proceeded to the airport. As they approached the airport, Jack passed a large sign that pointed straight ahead to the main terminal. Instead, he took a smaller road marked General Aviation that pointed to the right.

"Honey," Carole said, "the passenger terminal is straight ahead. You're going the wrong way."

"That's for regular passengers," he explained. "We are not on a commercial flight."

"What are we flying on?" She said with a puzzled look.

"An airplane owned by Potter Industries. We should be the only passengers on the plane. We get special treatment tonight. We will be going to Uncle Henry's funeral in style."

"I'm glad I had everybody wear their Sunday best," Carole commented.

Jack quickly parked the car. Of the three suitcases in the car, Jack took two and his wife picked up the other. "Carole," he said, "I can come back for that one."

Carole almost sounded insulted as she replied, "As much work as I do around the ranch, this is no problem." Jack did not argue.

They proceeded into the building set aside for passengers and owners flying on noncommercial aircraft. There, as they approached a large counter where pilots submitted flight plans, were two stewardesses. One held a printed sign that stated CURTIS.

"Hello, I'm Jack Curtis and this is my wife, Carole," he said. "We were unable to find babysitters on such short notice, so we had to bring the children along."

"That's alright, sir. I'm Holly and this is Sherry, and there is a bedroom on the plane where your children can quickly go to sleep if necessary."

"We are the hostesses for your flight and we are proud to be at your service," Sherry said, "and it is a pleasure to meet you."

Setting down the suitcases, Jack put his right hand up to the brim of his fedora, and said, "It is a pleasure to meet you ladies."

"Yes," said Carole. "I agree, after this hectic day it is good to see smiling faces." He and Carole shook hands with the two women

"These airport employees can take your luggage to the plane and if you will join us, we will proceed out onto the tarmac," Holly said.

Together the six of them walked out to the plane while the two airport loaders took the luggage to be stowed in the baggage section. "Just follow me," Sherry said, as she preceded Jack's family walking up the steps leading to the door of the airplane. Then, once inside, she said, "May I take your hat, sir?"

"Yes, thank you," Jack said handing her his fedora.

"Wow," Carole said, impressed at the airplane's fancy interior. "Are all airplanes like this one?"

"Not quite," Sherry said. Ignoring how the aircraft was luxuriously furnished, she simply said, "Most have far more seats and less leg room. We rarely have more than a dozen or so people on a flight. There is a bedroom to our immediate rear and restrooms fore and aft. There is also an office, complete with a typewriter and adding machine, where business can be conducted when necessary."

"We will be taking off shortly," Holly said. "We need each of you to take a seat and buckle your seat belts. As soon as we're airborne we can serve each of you a beverage or something to eat, as you wish."

"Wow," six-year-old David exclaimed as he took his seat. "This is neat!" The July sun had not yet set, so he could still observe the activity outside. Likewise, Liz held Mr. Giraffe up to her window so he could see also.

"Mrs. Curtis, your children are so well behaved," Holly commented. "And your little girl is just adorable."

"Thank you," Carole laughed. "But, be careful, we don't want you to give her a swelled head and big ego."

"I'm sure that could never happen, Mrs. Curtis," Holly said with a smile.

It occurred to Carole that it was the first time in her life people had repeatedly called her Mrs. Curtis. It was like she was suddenly no longer an ordinary person, and somehow more important than she had previously been. For a few moments she pondered that thought.

Chapter Three

As the plane took off, everyone could observe a beautiful sunset. Within a few moments, everyone was able to unbuckle their seat belts. Then, Holly returned and said, "Mr. Curtis, may I get you or your family something to eat or a beverage?"

"I'm hungry," young David said.

Carole rolled her eyes. "The bottomless pit speaks," she said. Then to David, she said, "You just ate less than an hour ago. How can you be hungry?"

"It's quite all right, ma'am," Holly replied. "I can heat a meal, for him, in our oven, or we have a selection of sandwiches available."

"I would like a hamburger, please," David said.

"You've got it, young man." Then turning to his parents, she said, "And for you folks?"

"I'll just have a cup of coffee," Carole said.

"And you, sir?" Holly asked.

"I think I'll have a beer," Jack replied.

"We have a selection of imported beers on board," Holly replied. "Any particular brand?"

"Whatever you bring will be perfect. I doubt if you stock the local brand, and I'm not picky."

Then, looking over at Liz, everyone noticed she was asleep. "I'm sure she would be much more comfortable in the bedroom," the hostess said.

"Yes," Jack said. "Lead the way, and I'll tuck her in." Then, picking up his daughter and cradling her in his arms, he followed Holly to the bedroom. Carole followed them.

"You even have a seatbelt across the bed," Carole noticed.

"Yes, ma'am. It's FAA regulations. Sometimes there is turbulence, and it is necessary."

Jack and Carole carefully took off Liz's shoes and dress and tucked her in with Mr. Giraffe next to her. They each kissed her on the forehead. Then they returned to their seats and enjoyed the flight. Jack and Carole drank their beverages and watched David devour his hamburger. After he had finished eating, David asked, "Can I go see the pilot?"

"Champ," Jack replied, "the pilot is a busy man, and the last thing he needs is a young boy bothering him."

"It will be quite all right, sir. Captain Collins won't mind at all," Sherry said. "With your permission, I'll take him to the cockpit."

After Jack agreed, Sherry led the boy up to the flight deck.

"David," she said. "this is our pilot, Captain Collins, and our co-pilot is Senior First Officer Miller."

"Well, hello, young man," the Pilot said. "Would you like to become a pilot someday?"

"Yes, sir!" the wide-eyed boy replied. "That would be neat."

"Well, step right up, and I can tell you a little about how this thing works."

"My father said you were busy, so I shouldn't bother you for very long," David sheepishly said.

"As you can see, there are two of us here, so your dad has nothing to fear, and I would be happy to tell you all about flying an airplane." With that, Captain Collins began to point out the instruments and describe their purpose. The three flight crew members seemed to enjoy the way the child was intrigued and mesmerized by the information.

After a while, the boy said, "Thank you, sir, but I better go now." He returned to his parents and exclaimed, "Daddy, I know how the plane flies!"

With a smile, Jack replied, "Easy, champ. I think it will take years of training and experience before you'll be ready to take the controls."

Meanwhile, in the cockpit, the SFO asked Sherry in a low voice, "Just between us, what's your first opinion of the new majority owners of Potter Industries?"

Sherry smiled. "So far, I'm very impressed. They seem very nice and have some of the best-behaved children I've ever seen. I think we will enjoy working for them a lot better than Henry Potter."

The SFO laughed. "That's not saying much. Dealing with anyone would be better than Old Man Potter. That was like working for the devil."

"That's true," Sherry agreed with a laugh. "But they seem like really good people. I think we will like working for them."

Despite David's euphoria about seeing the cockpit controls, he was shortly asleep, and Jack carried him into the bedroom and put him in bed next to his sister. Then, after securing the seatbelt across the bed, he returned to his wife. Holly brought them a blanket and two pillows. "I can bring more blankets, if you need them," she said.

"Thank you, Holly, this should be sufficient," Carole replied. She leaned her head over on her husband's shoulder, and the crew turned off the interior cabin lights. Once they were alone, Jack whispered, "What do you think, honey?"

"Truthfully, I'm a little scared," Carole admitted.

"Why is that, sweetheart?"

"We barely have enough money to make it until the cattle are sold each year, and now, you're talking about buying two new cars. I don't want to wind up with spoiled kids or us to become like the uppity snobs who flaunt wealth. I've always disliked those people. I don't want us to be like them."

"Sweetheart, I've always appreciated that you agreed with my thrifty nature. I think the biggest change is that I will no longer have to be a part-time security guard at the Masonite plant to make ends meet. We will take things one day at a time and adjust. I have no intention of showing off any signs of wealth. That might cause April to hound us to death."

"That's another thing that scares me, she might make life miserable for us," she said before going to sleep.

Jack put his arm around his wife and reflected on the past hours. He didn't consider himself scared, but he was apprehensive. He was worried that, like it or not, his life would change. He had to make sure it wasn't for the worse.

Jack woke up briefly as the plane landed in Chicago to refuel. Then, without waking up Carole, he asked Holly for their New York ETA. "Three A.M.," she replied. "And you must set your watch ahead an hour for Eastern Time when we arrive."

Knowing he would have a busy day ahead of him, he lay back with his head next to Carole's to try to get a little shut-eye. After he did, the two flight attendants agreed, "They seem like a perfect couple. I like them already."

Chapter Four

As the plane landed at Bedford Falls, Jack woke up, and as he pulled his arm from around Carole, who was cuddled up next to him, she was also awakened. Then, as the plane taxied to its parking area, Holly came to them and said, "There will be a limo waiting to take you to your hotel."

"Thank you, Holly. Carole and I will go get the kids."

The two of them quickly went and got their children dressed, and carried them to the plane's door. Before leaving, Jack thanked the pilot and the rest of the crew for the excellent flight. Then, after a little additional small talk, he and Carole went down the stairs to a waiting Limo.

A man in a suit introduced himself at the vehicle's door. Holding out his hand, he said, "I'm Harvey McClellan, Mr. Curtis, the interim president of Potter Industries. Welcome to Bedford Falls, New York."

With a smile, Jack shook the man's hand and said, "Call me Jack. When someone calls me Mr. Curtis, I look around for my late father. And, you are the company president?"

"Yes, Jack. Your uncle was chairman of the board, president, and CEO of Potter Industries. He micromanaged every facet of the business. During the reorganization, I have been designated interim president."

Where There Is Life There Is Always Hope

Two seats were facing each other in the limo. Jack, Carole, and the sleeping children were on the one facing forward while Mr. McClelland sat on the other. "The board of directors will meet at 10 a.m. to discuss possible changes to the company. The driver will take you to your suite at the Bedford Falls Hilton. Then we can return for you before the meeting after you've had some sleep."

"How long have you worked for my uncle, Harvey?"

"Twelve years" was the reply.

"Then, I presume, you would know about the company's profitability and future growth prospects," Jack said.

"Why, yes, that would be the case."

"Good! Come back for me at seven," Jack replied. "I need to be briefed on all of the aspects of the company beyond a simple balance sheet and P & L statement."

A look of surprise came over Harvey's face. "Most company officers assumed you would just sell your stock and leave for Texas." Then with a smile, he added, "Do you plan to stay for a while?"

"I have no idea what I am going to do yet," Jack replied. "But first, answer a question. Is Potter Industries profitable?"

"Yes, it is," Harvey answered emphatically.

"And, second, is it well run, with well-qualified people heading its operations?"

Harvey said with a big, proud smile, "Mr. Potter personally hired every one of us from an Ivy League college. I finished fifth in my class at Wharton."

"Then, I would be foolish to just sell my interests and leave. If everything you say is accurate and correct, I need to learn a great deal more. And I can do that talking with you tomorrow."

"I will look forward to it, Jack."

Jack held out his hand as the limo pulled up to the porte cochere of the hotel. "I'm impressed. Come back to pick me up at seven. Then we can go somewhere there's a lot of good coffee, and you can brief me properly before that board meeting."

"Consider it done, Jack, and it is a pleasure to meet you," Harvey said as Jack and his family got out of the vehicle. A bellhop came out to gather the suitcases, and with little David holding his mother's hand and Jack carrying Liz, who remained asleep, they checked into the hotel and were shown to the suite the company had reserved for them. Their suite was on the top floor.

As they walked in, Carole was impressed but managed to say nothing. Jack gave the bellhop four dollars as he took the suitcases off the cart he was pushing. "Thank you for everything," Jack said.

"You are welcome, sir," the bellhop replied.

After the bellhop left, Carole gasped. "This looks like an apartment," she said. "We've lived in houses smaller than this. I had to bite my tongue to keep from looking like some rube from the sticks who was overly impressed."

"Well, you are impressed, aren't you, sweetheart?" Jack asked with a smile.

"Of course," she replied. "But I didn't want to show it and look like the small-town girl I am. I need to be like you and put on a confident face that shows I know what I'm doing and belong here."

"You do belong here," her husband said. "We just aren't going to let it go to our heads. We will remember who we are and not let it change us. Now let's get some sleep."

They quickly got the children into bed, and then Carole asked, "Are you sure we can keep being who we are and not let money ruin us? I would never want to wind up like April."

"Carole, that money-grubbing witch drove Dewey to his grave. We will tell her she needs to get a job and stop living off others. We don't owe her a thing."

"I know. I get tired of April crying about her hard life when her bad luck is her fault. But when I think about how we put ourselves in financial jeopardy giving your brother money to keep her happy, it infuriates me," Carole commented.

"Then let's forget about April and go to bed. I need to try and get a little more sleep before six A.M."

"Good idea," Carole agreed.

Chapter Five

Jack Curtis received a wake-up call from the hotel lobby check-in desk at six A.M. He had gotten very little sleep after turning in. The questions he thought he needed to ask Harvey McClellan had occupied his mind. It was time to meet the day and see what awaited him. He kissed Carole and said, "Go back to sleep, sweetheart. You have the children to deal with."

"I wish I could go with you," she said.

"I do, too, but I'll take some good mental notes for you. I am nervous, but I am determined not to show it."

She kissed him again and said, "I have faith in you. With your way with words, you'll do just fine."

A short time later, the limo appeared outside the hotel, and Jack walked outside. The chauffeur opened the door for him. "Thank you," Jack said.

"You're welcome, sir," the chauffeur replied.

Harvey and another man were already in the limo. "This is Jeff Cooper," Harvey said as he introduced the second man. "He is the company's chief financial officer."

"It's a pleasure to meet you, Jeff," Jack said as they shook hands.

"The pleasure is all mine, Mr. Curtis," he replied.

"Please, call me Jack. That's what all the hands on my ranch call me, and I see no need to be any different here." In reality, he never had more than one or two people working for him part-time on his ranch, but he felt a need to appear as prosperous as possible. Then, with a smile, he added, "Is there somewhere we can get a bite to eat? I'm a little hungry."

"We have just the place," Harvey said. "There's a café with a small room where we sometimes go to talk business."

Soon, they were inside the café and had ordered breakfast. Jack asked his first question as they waited for breakfast to be served. "Tell me about my Uncle Henry. The only thing I know about him is my mother cursed a blue streak whenever she mentioned him."

Both men laughed. "Permission to speak freely?" Jeff asked.

"Yes, please do. I want the unvarnished truth."

"Well, Jack, your uncle was a hard man to work for." Harvey paused, "We called him the robber baron from Hell. If there was a death in someone's family, he never gave the employee time off. They had to take time for the funeral unpaid. Most employees hope they can continue the policy and tradition and be excused from attending his funeral."

"Permission granted," Jack laughed. "My mother would want us to keep Uncle Henry happy."

"Well, if he's happy, it will be the first time that's ever happened that I know of," Jeff commented.

The waitress brought the men the meals they had ordered. They ate as they continued their conversation.

"What other businesses run the economy here in Bedford Falls?" Jack curiously asked.

"Potter Industries and our manufacturing facilities employ at least three-quarters of the people around here. There are a lot of small businesses that employ the rest. Potter wanted to own everything. But there was a place that provided options for those who wanted to work elsewhere." Harvey explained. "Almost all the mom-and-pop businesses from the Studebaker dealership to this restaurant began with money borrowed from the Bailey Building and Loan," Harvey explained.

Jeff added, "Between those small businesses and the home loans George Bailey provided, I suspect over ninety percent of local citizens are shareholders in Bailey's Building and Loan."

"George Bailey sounds like an extraordinary fellow," Jack commented.

"It's a David and Goliath story, really," Harvey said. "Potter tried for years to run George Bailey out of business, but Bailey always got the better of him. There is a real estate development west of town called Bailey Acres. Bailey gave loans that allowed people to buy homes and not live in the overpriced town homes Potter rented out."

After a sip of coffee, Harvey continued. "You've heard of the Levittown communities?"

"Yes, I have," Jack replied.

"Well, before Levittown, there was Bailey Acres. William Levitt mass-produced what George Bailey was already doing."

After another bite of eggs and a drink of coffee, Jeff continued. "There is an interesting legend I wouldn't dare mention if Potter were alive." Jeff looked around to ensure no one would overhear what he was saying. "If he caught anyone mentioning the story, they were fired." He paused. "Maybe, I shouldn't mention it now." He rubbed his hand across the back of his neck.

"Go ahead, Harv. Potter's dead. Jack here might enjoy the story." Jeff commented. "I won't tell anyone."

"Well, it happened before I came to Bedford Falls," Jeff began, "But the old-timers call it the Christmas miracle of '45. I've heard several versions, but the story goes that thousands of dollars mysteriously went missing from the Building and Loan, and Potter called the authorities and demanded Bailey's arrest. The pressure was so much that, apparently, Bailey decided to kill himself. But first he went to a bar and got drunk."

Harvey shook his head and said, "Here's where the story gets a little strange. It seems that after getting inebriated, Bailey imagined an angel showed up and talked him out of killing himself. Meanwhile, Bailey's friends spread the word he was in trouble, and people showed up with the money to repay the missing funds. Finally, the bank examiners left, and Bailey spent the next few years paying everyone back, and his building and loan is still as profitable as ever. And George Bailey continued to give Potter nightmares until Potter passed on last Sunday."

"That's amazing!" Jack said. "I wonder what happened to the missing money in the first place."

"Nobody knows," Harvey said. "Many people accused Potter of taking it, but I can't imagine even him being that low."

"He was that low, Harv," Jeff said bluntly.

"How's that?"

"Only a half dozen of us know, but the original company accountant, Mike Singleton, told me it was $8,000, and Potter stole it. Mike said he used the information to extort favors from Potter until he died a few years later. With Mike dead, the rest of us had no proof, so we kept our mouths shut to keep our jobs."

"Oh, my gosh! Potter was even a bigger dirt bag than I suspected," Harvey exclaimed. "I wonder what he used the money for."

"I'm sure it was for something nefarious. The man made a career out of evicting widows and orphans."

"How much is that money worth with interest today?" Jack inquired.

"Eight thousand dollars at five percent interest over fifteen years would be about sixteen thousand dollars," the financial officer explained.

"Make out a check for that amount to George Bailey, and I'll deliver it," Jack said. "List it as a repayment for a loan from 1945. Let's not sully our company founder's name, even if he deserved it."

"I can do that," Jeff said. "The less said, the better."

From there, the conversation turned to more traditional business topics as Jack examined the company's balance sheet and profit and loss paperwork while the two company men described the products manufactured by Potter Industries.

"Has there been any discussion about Potter Industries diversifying into other fields of business and enterprise?" Jack asked.

"There has been some discussion in the past, but Potter's reputation was so horrible others were hesitant to deal with him. No one would consider selling their business to him. From time to time, someone would work with Potter if they thought they could make a buck, but they often came to regret it. Potter's business was profitable, but other major business owners in New York have not trusted the man during this past decade. Consequently, business growth has been slow and inconsistent."

"That would be understandable," Jack agreed.

"I probably should have mentioned this before, but you need to know how your Uncle Henry structured his estate," Jeff Cooper said.

"Yes, I've been meaning to ask about that," Jack replied. His confident smile belied the fact that previously he had no such thought.

"Fred Rosenberg will meet with you later to provide exact details, but since estate taxes go as high as seventy-seven percent, a trust held almost all of Potter's assets. The trust includes fifty-two percent of all company stock, real estate, and other assets. As a result of this trust, you will incur no taxes beyond the usual taxes owed on income paid to you directly from the trust."

Jack continued to bluff that he knew more about high finance than he did by saying, "I had assumed that would be the case. Back home, Jim Filbert has encouraged me to set up a trust or similar financial entity."

After breakfast, Jack went with the two men to view some of the company's manufacturing facilities. Potter Industries had a garment factory that produced women's clothing. A second factory also produced small kitchen appliances and radios for national retailers.

Chapter Six

Finally, at ten A.M., Jack was present for the board of directors meeting of Potter Industries. Usually held the third Friday of each month, this was a special session required to restructure the company due to Potter's death.

Unknown to Jack, four board members met earlier to discuss the future of Potter Industries. They were Phillip Gallagher, Bill McClusky, Tim Murrey, and Ethel Thomasson.

Gallagher spoke first. "I think it would be best to encourage this Texas cowboy to return home. We don't need outsiders involved in our local affairs. I think we can buy him out easily."

"Why don't we get to know him first?" Tim asked. "A little new blood might help the corporation."

"I think Phil is right," Bill replied. "With Potter dead and the recession ending, we should be on the verge of increased profitability. Potter's greed has held us back for years. With him gone, we could be looking at better days ahead. We don't need to share it with an outsider."

"Right!" Gallagher responded. "This morning, his shares are worth about thirty-one million dollars. If we acquire them and go public with an IPO, they could be worth triple that in a year. So, I figure he will jump at it if we offer him a generous amount of thirty-three million dollars for his shares. Then we can do what we wish with no outside interference." After some discussion, they decided to make Jack the offer.

As the board meeting began, Congressman McCluskey and state senator Murrey were seated at the table. Each owned five percent of the company stock. The general manager of the Bedford Falls National Bank, Phillip Gallagher, who owned an additional five percent, was also there. While Potter Industries owned the bank, its general manager had been allowed to become another of the company's shareholders, with the remaining thirty-three percent held as treasury stock.

Jeff Cooper was on the board, as was the mayor of Bedford falls, Patrick O'Reilly. Mrs. Ethel Thomasson, who had served as Henry Potter's secretary for years, rounded out the group as the board's secretary. Jack had briefly met and shook hands with each of them before the meeting.

As interim company president, Harvey McClellan was on hand as a non-voting member to answer questions. He directed Jack to the seat at the head of the table.

After everyone was seated, Harvey rose and said, "It is my pleasure to officially introduce Mr. Jack Curtis from Texas." Everyone acknowledged Jack with a nod and a hello.

Jack smiled and proceeded as though he were chairing the Cattleman's Association Meeting back home. "I have had a chance to meet and shake hands with all of you, and I can see that the company is doing well, and I am confident that will continue to be the case." Then, Jack said, "Mrs. Thomasson is there an agenda for the meeting?"

"Yes, the first order is to read the minutes from the last time we met," she replied.

"Since this is a special confab, I move that the reading of those minutes be postponed until the next regular session," Congressman McClusky said.

"So moved," Jack concurred. After a second, Jack looked around. "Any discussion on the motion?" No one spoke up. "Seeing none, those in favor of the motion, say aye." Everyone voted in the affirmative.

Jack looked at the board secretary. "Mrs. Thomasson, what is the next item on the agenda?"

"The election of the new corporate board chairman."

"If I may make a suggestion," Jack said, "before we move to that item, I think we need a motion to designate Harvey McClellan as the official company president instead of continuing as the interim president."

"So moved," Jeff said.

"Do I hear a second?"

"Second," Mayor O'Reilly affirmed.

After the quick, symbolic action of a unanimous vote, Jack shook hands with the new company president and said, "Congratulations, Harvey."

"Thanks, Jack."

Bank president Gallagher said, "May I be recognized before moving on to the regular agenda, Mr. Curtis?"

"Certainly, sir," Jack replied. "The floor is yours, and please call me Jack."

Mr. Gallagher rose with a big smile, "I'm sure you are anxious to get back home, so after checking to verify the current stock price this morning, I found what stock you currently hold is worth 30.4 million dollars. Therefore, to simplify matters and allow you to return home, we are prepared to offer you thirty-three million dollars for the inherited business interests."

With a look combining surprise and shock, Jack said without hesitation, "That is most generous of you, and I appreciate it. However, Mr. McClellan and Mr. Cooper have assured me the company is profitable, and my uncle only hired people from prestigious universities. Down in Texas, we have a saying that anyone who sells a profitable business without first seeing what he can do with it is not very smart. Therefore, I have to decline your very kind offer. But I do thank you."

Looking at Mrs. Thomasson, Jack said, "I suppose we need to move on to the next item; electing a new board chairman."

State senator Murray said, "I would nominate Mr. Gallagher."

"Second the motion," Ethel Thomasson said.

With a big smile, Jack asked, "Are there any additional nominations?" Then, after a moment of silence, he repeated, "Do I hear other nominations?"

"I nominate Jack Curtis," Jeff Cooper said boldly.

With another big smile, Jack said, "Do I hear a second?"

"Second the motion," Gallagher said reluctantly. Then, he quickly added, "I request my name be removed from nomination and move that we elect Jack Curtis as the new board chairman by acclamation." Jack's election as board chairman was then quickly made official.

"Before we adjourn," Jack said, "I suggest we consider a new name for the corporation. With my uncle's death, it might help us better prepare for the future. While flying into this beautiful city, I noticed a large lake to the east. What's the name of the lake?"

"That is Lake Cayuga," the congressman stated.

"While I am open to other suggestions, I would suggest Cayuga National Industries as a new name for the company. What does everyone else think?"

"We're not a national corporation," Murrey noted.

"Not yet," Jack agreed. "However, it would be a move for future planning."

"My constituents would love it," McCluskey replied. "I move we accept."

After the board accepted the new name, the meeting ended. Jack excused himself to see to other matters, and Jeff walked him to the waiting limo. "Congratulations, Jack," Jeff said as the chauffeur opened the door. "I'm happy you decided not to sell. I don't know what Gallagher and his friends have in mind, but I've never trusted any of them."

"Thanks, Jeff. I hope I haven't fallen into a snake pit. That bank manager didn't seem very happy with me." With that, Jack had the chauffeur take him back to the hotel with orders to return at two for his meeting with lawyer Rosenberg.

Chapter Seven

It was not until Jack was alone in the elevator returning to the suite where he and Carole were staying, that he felt he could relax. He had spent the entire morning acting like he knew what he was doing. Now Jack exhaled to release the tension he had tried so hard to conceal all morning. He also said a silent prayer that he had not said anything to expose the truth about how financially broke he was.

For six hours, he had presented himself as a prosperous rancher who was the board chairman of the Tri-county Cattleman's Association. But, in reality, he was not a person of wealth. The money he had given his invalid brother-in-law and the current economic recession had left him close to bankruptcy.

If two days before, someone had offered to pay him thirty-three million dollars for some stock he had just inherited, he would have screamed yes before they could change their mind. However, just thirty minutes ago, he had refused that exact amount. The corporate board had been too anxious to buy his new stock. He suspected he might do much better in the future.

As he exited the elevator and opened the door to their suite, Carole said, "Thank heavens you're here. If you were gone much longer, I might have gone nuts."

"I'm sorry, sweetheart," he said as he kissed her. "I'll get you out of here after lunch. I have an appointment with Fred

Rosenberg at 2:30, and I want you to be with me while I meet with him."

"That's the best news I've heard all morning," she replied.

"Remember, Carole: we're rich ranchers from Texas. That bluff worked this morning, and you have to help me maintain the image."

His wife laughed. "I know that's what April thinks, but how did you sell that story here?"

With the confident smile he had used all morning, Jack explained, "I'm a rancher from Texas, and I am the chairman of the board of the Tri-county Cattleman's Association. I never lied. Everything I told them was the truth."

Carole laughed again. "You took Bob Murdock's place on the board as a favor to him and four months ago, you missed a meeting. So, they elected you board chairman that day since you weren't there to say no. Am I missing anything?"

"No, sweetheart, you're not. But before I tell you about how my morning went, please tell me about yours."

"Well, let's see," she began sarcastically. "Fortunately, the kids slept late, but it got mentally stimulating after that. We watched *Romper Room*, then *Captain Kangaroo* and then cartoons featuring Crusader Rabbit. Those were the high points of my morning. Finally, I'm ready to go home where I can accomplish something worthwhile."

"Sweetheart, let's get some lunch, and afterward, I'll get you out of this hotel room. I think you will like what you hear."

After they got the kids ready, they went to the restaurant on the first floor. Jack told her what had transpired that morning. After he mentioned the offer the board had made him for his stock, Carole was shocked.

"Honey, you turned down thirty-three million dollars!" she exclaimed. "Why?"

"Shhh," he cautioned. "Keep your voice down. We don't know whose listening. When we see the lawyer in a couple of hours, I think you will see why."

"I hope so. I don't want to think you've lost your mind," Carole commented.

"Sweetheart, as quick as they were to offer me that money, I suspected the stock might be worth a lot more in the future."

"I hope so," she agreed.

After eating lunch, they had their driver take them to a nursery where they dropped off the kids, and then the chauffeur took them to the office of Fred Rosenberg.

"Mr. Curtis, it's good to finally meet you in person." Rosenberg said.

"Thank you, and it's great to meet you as well. And please call me Jack." Then, with a big smile, he added, "My mother named me John, but I always liked Jack much better. And I'd like to introduce my wife, Carole."

"It's a pleasure to meet you," Carole said.

"The pleasure is all mine, Carole," the lawyer said as he shook hands with the two of them. "Please have a seat, and I will go over the specifics of your uncle's will." He paused. "A lot of clients like a stiff drink while doing business—especially New York businessmen," he smiled. "So, we have an eight-year-old Scotch available as well as coffee."

"It's a little early in the day for us for the first one, but some coffee would be nice, Mr. Rosenberg," Jack answered.

"I'll order that, and please call me Fred." He punched a button on his intercom and said, "Betty, please bring some coffee for our clients." The secretary stated she would be right there.

The lawyer began to explain the details of Henry Potter's will. "The bulk of his estate is in a trust which, in addition to company stock worth a little under thirty-one million dollars, also contains some thirty million in real estate, art, and other assets. You now control the trust, which provides an annual income averaging six hundred twenty thousand dollars a year if the trust remains intact."

Having been warned by Jack prior to the meeting not to be impressed by dollar amounts, Carole suppressed her desire to gasp and somehow managed to sit quietly. It was not easy.

"In addition," Fred continued, "there is a checking account. It contains about sixty thousand dollars, the exemption amount not subject to estate taxes. As the beneficiary, you can go to the Bedford Falls National Bank and have no problem transferring the account into your name."

Jack nodded.

The lawyer continued, "I understand you turned down thirty-three million for the stock this morning. May I ask why?"

"I figured if they were willing to offer more than it was worth, maybe I should keep it. But I have a question."

"Go ahead, and I'll answer it," Rosenberg said.

"In addition to the stock I now own, who else owns stock in the company?" Jack inquired.

"There are two politicians Henry allowed to own stock as a sort of payoff for doing his bidding and getting him what he wanted. I understand they each have five percent. Also, Gallagher, who has always done Henry's dirty work at the bank, has an additional five. That man has foreclosed on more widows and orphans than a Charles Dickens character. The rest is held as treasury stock." Rosenberg allowed Jack and Carole to comprehend that information for a second and continued. "The only friends Henry Potter ever had were Gallagher and that old bat that served as his secretary. I understand her job was to spy on others and tell Potter whom he needed to fire. She assigned others to push his wheelchair after his prior gopher retired. She will retire herself when she turns sixty-five in a few months."

"I'm glad I got the company's name changed," Jack mentioned.

"Yes, I heard about that. I'm curious about why you did that?"

"After how Mother talked about Uncle Henry, I didn't want to continue to own anything with his name on it. I hate to sound petty, but that's how I felt."

The lawyer laughed. "That's the consensus around here. The other board members were going to pick a new name for the business. You just beat them to it."

After more talk about the Bedford Falls area, Jack and Carole thanked the lawyer for everything and went to the bank. There they got two thousand dollars in small bills (tens and twenties). He gave his wife half of the money before returning to the limo. Then, Jack reached into a compartment beside the seat and pulled out a telephone. He asked for the mobile operator to connect him to Jeff Cooper's office.

"This car has a phone!" Carole gasped. "We can make calls from the car?"

"Yes, dear, but don't use it to call the folks back home. I understand these mobile calls are very expensive," he said as he put his hand over the phone.

Jeff answered the call. "Yes, Jack, what can I do for you?"

"Where is the mortuary that has Uncle Henry's body? I need to see about his funeral."

"He's at the Knickerbocker Brothers Funeral Home. It's over at Fifth and Main. Tomorrow is a graveside service since the only people there will be your family and Bishop Morgan of Saint James Episcopal Church. We also had to hire pallbearers." Jeff laughed. "I hope I can be excused from attending."

"Permission granted," Jack laughed. "I will be there as a family obligation. I'm guessing the minister is also being paid for his services."

Jeff laughed again. "Yes, he is. I doubt even a man of the cloth would go to Henry Potter's funeral as an act of Christian charity."

As the limo proceeded to the mortuary, Carole remarked, "Honey, it is so sad people could dislike anyone as badly as your uncle."

Chapter Eight

On the way to the funeral parlor, Carole asked, "When you set up the new account, why didn't you put my name on it along with yours?"

"That new account was to transfer the money to our bank at home. When we return home, your name will be on the account then. The less I have to do here in New York, the better."

His wife gave him a peck on the cheek and said, "I didn't say anything in the bank because you gave me half the money you received. I think that is the most money I've ever held in my hand at one time."

Jack looked his wife in the eyes and commented, "We don't want to be in the habit of carrying a lot of money around. The way the world is, it could be dangerous."

"At least I get to enjoy it for a little while," she giggled.

Once inside the mortuary they met the funeral director, who led them to a small alcove on the left side of the building's chapel. There he opened the lid of a silver and blue casket. Henry F. Potter was an obese eighty-year-old man with a perpetual scowl. Jack turned away. "I never met him," he said aloud. "I hate to say it, but he looks about like I imagined he might."

"Mr. Curtis," the funeral director said, "His office scheduled a graveside service for ten tomorrow morning. Is that still your intention?"

"Yes, my wife and I will meet Bishop Morgan and the pallbearers at the cemetery." Looking around, Jack added, "I understand you had to hire them."

"Yes, I regret to say that was the case," the mortician answered. "Unfortunately, Mr. Potter was not the most popular man in Bedford Falls."

As they were leaving the building, Jack turned to his wife and said, "Now I know why Uncle Henry left his fortune to me."

"Why was that, honey?"

"So, there would be someone to feel obligated to attend his funeral."

Carole laughed. "I'm happy he needed a mourner. Now maybe we don't have to pinch pennies anymore."

"Just the same, sweetheart, we don't want to flaunt wealth. That could cause a lot of problems and attract people we don't want around us."

"No problem, honey," Carole replied. "When I'm out in public I'll pretend we're still broke, if I can wear a mink stole at home."

As they were getting back in the limo, Jack laughed and replied, "I'll do my best to see that you are always well provided for."

The final place Jack wanted to go for the day was the Bailey Building and Loan. He and Carole entered the building holding hands, looking forward to ending the long day. In his pocket was a check Jeff had printed earlier for sixteen thousand dollars. After it would be delivered, Jack could relax.

Walking up to a desk to the right of the tellers, Jack requested to see George Bailey. The man walked over to an office and said, "There's someone to see George; he says it is very important."

A young man who appeared to be in his mid-twenties came out and said, "I'm Pete Bailey, how may I help you."

"My name is Jack Curtis and this is my wife, Carole. I really need to speak with your father. It's a matter which others should have resolved many years ago."

"Dad had a heart attack recently and the doctors have ordered him to take it easy and rest," the young man said.

"It sounds like your father could use some good news, and I have some information I believe will make his day. I hope he is up to receiving visitors, because this is very good news," Jack disclosed while shaking hands.

"It would help if I knew what this referred to," Pete said.

"Long story short, sir. It is about an apology he is entitled to but is not expecting. I need to deliver it to rectify a wrong of many years ago."

"Well, Dad could use some good news." Pete agreed.

"Believe me," Jack said. "I want to brighten up his day. This should be the best news he has received in a while. Hopefully, you can direct me to him."

The young man looked stunned. "I'll write down the address for you. Then I will call and tell Dad you are coming."

"Thank you." Jack took the paper and returned to the car. The Chauffeur then drove to the address.

Pete phoned his father. "Dad, some guy in a chauffeur-driven limo came in saying he had some good news and an apology for you. He insisted on seeing you. I gave him your address."

His father stuttered slightly as he said, "Who, ah, who was he?"

"I don't know. I've never seen him before. He introduced himself as Jack Curtis and he was here with his wife. He also said something about owing you an apology. He's on his way to your place."

"Thanks, son. I guess I'll meet him at the door when he gets here," George replied.

Looking out the window, George Bailey saw the large, black limo pull up to the curb. Two people got out and walked to the door.

"George!" his wife exclaimed. "George, you are supposed to be resting. You need to listen to the doctor."

"Relax Mary, I'm not an invalid and I feel fine. I refuse to stay in bed all day."

As Jack and Carole approached the door George wanted to open it over his wife's objections. She reprimanded him by saying, "You need to listen to the doctor. You sit down and I'll get the door."

As his wife continued to protest, George shook hands with Jack as he entered and said, "You must be Jack Curtis, I'm George Bailey and my son called and said it was urgent that you meet with me."

"Yes, Mr. Bailey—"

"Call me George," Bailey said as he interrupted Jack.

"Okay, but you must call me Jack and this is my wife, Carole. And we are here to correct a terrible injustice."

George's wife immediately said, "I am Mary Bailey, and this stubborn husband of mine needs to sit down. The doctor said he was not to exert himself."

Mary quickly had her way and shortly the four of them were sitting in the living room, where Jack began to explain the purpose for the visit.

"What is this all about?" Mary asked.

Jack began at the beginning, explaining how the day before he learned that an uncle he had never met had passed away leaving his fortune to him. He continued. "After getting here and learning about the company my Uncle Henry founded, I discovered that fifteen years ago eight thousand dollars of your money somehow wound up in my uncle's hands. I am ashamed and embarrassed that he never returned it, and with interest and inflation it is worth double that amount today. So, I am hoping you will accept my sincerest apologies as well as this check." He handed the check to George.

George sat speechless for a number of seconds and his wife said, "Well, say thank you, George."

George was clearly stunned as he said, "Well, ah, well, ah, ah, thank you. I never expected this." After gaining his composure he asked, "Where are you folks from?"

"We're live near Wall, Texas, which ironically is little more than a hole in the wall," Jack joked.

"Well, thank you again," George repeated. Then after some additional conversation, Jack and Carole returned to their limo.

After the driver returned to the hotel, he got out, opening the door and Jack said, "I'm sorry, I haven't asked you what your name is."

"Tom, sir, Tom Munson," the chauffeur replied.

"Are you married, Tom?"

"Yes, Mr. Curtis, we have four children," Tom replied.

"Well, Tom, thank you for the excellent job you do. Here is a little token of my appreciation. Take your family out tonight and have fun." He handed Tom two twenty-dollar bills as he extended his hand.

"Thank you, sir, thank you very much!" the chauffeur said as he shook Jack's hand enthusiastically.

As they returned to their room, Carole said, "It's obvious your uncle never did anything like that. You must admit, honey, forty dollars is a lot of money."

"I know, sweetheart, but it seemed like something I should do."

Chapter Nine

George and Mary Bailey sat quietly for several seconds after Jack and Carole left their home. They were still stunned by the friendly visit and the windfall of money. Finally, George and Mary began to discuss what had just happened. As he looked at the check, George said, "Mary, if that young man is not the antithesis of Henry Potter, I can't imagine who is."

"We now know what happened to the money," Mary said. "Potter stole it, just like everyone always figured."

"Yes," George agreed, "but a lot of people also suspected Uncle Billy." With tears in his eyes he added, "The poor man was hounded by the knowledge he lost the money until the day he died in 1950."

"Your Uncle Billy can rest in peace now," Mary commented. "Everyone will now know he was innocent." She laughed, "Absent-minded, but innocent."

"I can tell Pete that this was good news indeed, but with Henry Potter dead who is there to battle with in the future?" George mused.

"There will be someone," Mary commented. "There always is." Then walking to the window, she added, "They seem like such a nice young couple. We should have them over for dinner sometime."

* * *

On Wednesday morning, Jack and Carole got dressed and took the children to breakfast. Young David complained, "Mom said we would get to see the Statue of Liberty."

"Davy, Mommy didn't know the Statue of Liberty would be 200 miles from where we were staying," Carole apologized.

"Relax sweetheart," Jack said. "When I'm finished with my work here, we will go to the Big Apple and see the sights, including the Statue of Liberty." He turned to his son, and said, "Your mother told you the truth, David. She just didn't know which day we would go."

"Neato!" the young boy exclaimed.

Carole turned toward her husband, winked and mouthed the words, "Thanks, honey."

At ten A.M. the family met the Episcopal bishop and the hearse at the cemetery. The six men who had been paid to perform the duty as pallbearers carried the coffin from the hearse to the grave and promptly left. There were two cemetery workers who would lower the coffin into the grave, along with Jack's family and the Right Reverend Morgan.

Bishop Morgan gave a short prayer and then spoke for ten minutes about how we must overlook the faults of others and leave judgments to God. He finished with, "As we commend the body of Henry Potter to the earth, from which we all sprang and must someday return, we are thankful for the salvation that God has provided for us all. We ask for His guidance and inspiration to always live a good life and to be kind to others. Amen."

Jack walked over and shook hands with Bishop Morgan and handed him twenty dollars. "Your company already compensated me," the reverend said.

"This is an extra thank-you for the nice words. Many people in this town I've spoken with would claim he didn't deserve it," Jack explained. "I think it is sad he treated so many people as he did."

"Well," said the cleric, "he has gone to his reward, and we need to leave judgments to God."

"Yes, Reverend, I agree. Thanks again." Jack replied.

"You are very welcome."

From there, the chauffeur took Jack and his family to the company headquarters. Upon arriving there, Carole admonished the children to behave themselves. "We are going to see the business that your daddy owns. If you are good, we will get you some ice cream tomorrow when we see the Statue of Liberty."

"Oh boy!" said David.

"I want strawberry!" Liz exclaimed.

"If you behave yourself, you can have all the strawberry ice cream you want tomorrow," their mother promised.

"Do I have to eat my vegetables, too?" the little girl asked with a frown.

"We'll get you extra ice cream, if you do," Carole replied.

They walked to Harvey's office. Jack made some mental notes about the appearance of the building as he did. He knocked on Harvey's office door and opened it and said, "Got a moment, Harv?"

"Absolutely, come on in."

"I'm taking the family to New York City and wanted to touch base with you first," Jack said.

"The company plane is waiting for you," Harvey said.

"Since this is a personal trip, I won't do it on the company dime," Jack explained. "I'll get a commercial flight to the big city and back. But I will use the company plane to return home Friday morning."

"I'm impressed, Jack," Harvey said with a smile.

"I don't want to be accused of hindering company profitability. Meanwhile, let me introduce my family," He quickly introduced Carole and his children.

Harvey shook hands with Carole and the two kids and said, "Just let me know when the limo needs to pick you up Friday morning, and I'll have it waiting for you," Harvey said.

"I was noticing there seems to be some maintenance and upkeep needed on the building."

"Yes, that cheap rotten son of a—" Harvey hesitated as he noticed Jack's children and continued, "—gun Potter let things deteriorate. We need to put some money into fixing up."

"Well, you have my permission. Go for it," Jack replied. "Also, I'm going to set my pay as board chairman at a dollar a year for now."

"What!" Both Harvey and Carole said in surprise.

"With the trust income, we are more than provided for," Jack explained. Then turning to Carole, he added, "This way, when April wants money, you can tell her we can't afford it since your husband makes only a dollar a year."

"Who's April?" Harvey asked as Carole started laughing.

"The widow of my late step-brother" He explained. "I'm tired of her using my family for a piggy bank."

Soon afterward the Curtis family was flying into Idlewild Airport. This side trip with the family was needed. The past two days Jack had been very self-conscious. He had felt as though all eyes were on him and he had to watch every word he said and every move he made. Now he could let his hair down and relax with his family.

They visited the Statue of Liberty and a few other sights, and on Thursday they went to Madison Square Garden to see the world-famous Ringling Brothers, Barnum and Bailey Circus. By early evening the exhausted children were asleep and Jack and Carole finally had time to themselves to discuss the past few days.

"Well, sweetheart, what do you think?" Jack asked his wife.

"I'm worried," she said truthfully. "The country club set in Austin and Dallas will see us as nouveau riches and the people like April will hound us for money. It will be hard to just be ordinary people anymore."

"We'll always be the same people we were a week ago, sweetheart. The difference is, now we have a little more money."

"But, now deadbeats like April will be even more insistent that we help them out." Carole replied.

"After we pay for Dewey's funeral, I figure we don't owe April anything. We can tell her to get a job," Jack said with a growl.

Chapter Ten

It was a bright, sunny afternoon in Bedford Falls. George looked at his wife Mary and said, "Twenty-eight years ago we were cheated out of a trip for our honeymoon by a bank run on the building and loan. We used the money to save the business. How would you like to take that trip today?"

"George, the doctor told you to rest," Mary argued.

"I can't think of a better rest than a long vacation, where we can see the places that we've always dreamed of. Mary, we've spent our lives helping others. Maybe it's time to take a little time for ourselves. And, we have the money to do it," he explained, as he held up the check.

"What about the kids?" Mary asked.

George laughed. "You know as well as I do, they're not kids anymore, Mary. They'll be happy for us. Besides, Pete has wanted to take over management of the building and loan. Maybe it's time to let him show what he can do."

"Are you sure about this, George?"

"I am the surest that I have ever been about anything. Let's do it." He smiled to await her reply.

"Okay. I suppose it's time to see life beyond Bedford Falls. Where should we go first?"

"I'm thinking we travel to Britain, then cruise down the Rhine River. Then to Paris, Rome, Greece, Spain. Why not see them all? Let's do it."

"Call a travel agency and I'll inform the kids that we'll be gone for a couple of weeks," Mary said gleefully.

Despite Mary's insistence that George relax while she packed and made arrangements for their things to be taken care of for two weeks, he convinced her to drive him to the building and loan at closing time.

Once there, he called the employees together and announced, "My wife has decided that we need a long vacation, so I have decided to step down from management and, subject to the approval of the board, I am suggesting my son Pete be promoted to be the new manager of our building and loan."

The other employees cheered and offered congratulations. Pete hugged his father and said, "I intend to make you proud, Dad."

* * *

The flight back to San Angelo was uneventful. Carole was no longer in awe of the well-furnished airplane as she considered the future. She was now aware that their financial circumstances would definitely change for the better in the immediate future. "I'm worried," she told Jack, as she leaned her head on his shoulder.

"Why, Carole? Things will work out fine. You'll see."

"I hope so," she replied. "If people think we're rich, I hate to think about how many people will have their hands out wanting us to give them a loan."

Jack smiled. "Just tell them your husband only inherited some stock. Tell everybody the board chairmanship is a ceremonial position where I earn a dollar a year and very little else has changed."

"I love the fact that we no longer have to worry about money, but do you really think we can continue to pretend we are still ordinary folks just getting by?" she pondered.

"Sweetheart, just remember that we are just ordinary folks. We just happened to come into a little money. We will continue to live frugally and not flaunt money," Jack explained.

Carole laughed. "You said we were going to get new cars for both of us when we get home. Won't that tip off people that our financial status has changed?"

"Sweetheart, the vehicles we have are falling apart. It should be obvious we need new cars. We don't have to buy Cadillacs. Something more reasonable will do."

"I hope you're right. I guess we'll see," she agreed.

* * *

One of the tellers in the Bailey Building and Loan brought it to Pete Bailey's attention that Mrs. O'Malley was late with her loan payment again. "This is two months in a row," she said.

"How Did dad always keep the old lady's payments on time, so she didn't fall behind?" Pete asked.

"He always drove by and collected it personally," the teller replied.

Pete sighed. "This is the twentieth century. We shouldn't have to do that. I'm going to prepare a letter to all shareholders that late payments will require a two-dollar late fee in the future."

"But Mr. Bailey, we've never charged late fees in the past," she replied.

"Paula, he replied, "this is a business and we need to run it like one. It would be ridiculous for us to drive around collecting payments from everyone like some sort of numbers runner."

"Very well, I'll call her and tell her that in the future late payments will cost her two dollars."

Pete then went to work preparing a list of items that would cost additional fees for shareholders in the future. "Dad was way too nice," Pete said. "It was no wonder we always lived in genteel poverty as I was growing up."

* * *

Three days after their return from New York, Jack got a call from a reporter for the *Tri-county Times*. "Mr. Curtis," he asked, "we have received a call from some town in New York that you have inherited a company named Cayuga National Industries, which along with an accompanying trust is worth a total of over sixty million dollars."

"Who in the world called and told you that?" Jack laughed. "He said his name was Gallagher and he said you should be congratulated," the reporter said.

Jack was determined not to sound irritated or angry. He realized he might not be able to fly under the radar as he had hoped. So, he took a deep breath and explained, "All I did was inherit some stock. That inheritance allowed me to gain the ceremonial position of board chairman for which I will earn a dollar a year. I have no idea how things will go in the future, but there is an excellent company president named Harvey McClellan and he can tell you more about the company than I can. I'm just a country boy who tries to run a local ranch."

Despite his efforts to downplay his new status, the paper published a front-page story two days later which read: Local Rancher Inherits National Company. The story went into detail that a call to company president McClellan was answered with "no comment" and Jack had claimed to know little about his inherited possessions. Public records, however, detailed the size of the new acquisitions Jack now had ownership of, and the paper accurately listed everything.

It was enough to make Jack curse up a storm. Nobody was going to buy his story of only earning a dollar a year now. There would be no flying under the financial radar in the future. For the first time in his life he cussed freedom of the press.

Chapter Eleven

Jack and Carole had always called their sister-in-law the Wicked Witch of the West. April Curtis used a car instead of a broom to travel, and she was not a happy person. Her life had been a succession of toxic and dysfunctional relationships. The last one had been a ten-year marriage to Jack's stepbrother Dewey. Now, April was in Carole's living room screaming.

"My second cousin, Betty Jean Porter, works at the bank and she says you people got over two hundred thousand dollars from a Henry F. Potter Trust, and now this paper says you are worth sixty million dollars." She held up the newspaper. "I could use a little help."

"We don't owe you anything, April," Carole replied.

Jack, who had been feeding cattle, had seen the big Cadillac coming up the road and hurried to the house, getting there after April arrived. He went inside and stepped between the two women. "Your champagne taste on a beer budget bankrupted Dewey. I've paid your incurred bills, and I don't want you bothering us anymore."

"Well, ain't that a fine how-do-you-do!" April screeched. "Big, rich, important people don't want to share the wealth and help their poor relatives."

As Jack argued with April, Carole left the room briefly and returned with a checkbook. She began writing in it.

"Get a job, April!" Jack demanded.

"The rich have no pity on the poor. That's the way the world has always been. I need to pay for that new car of mine."

"Get a job, April!" Jack repeated.

Carole stepped over to her husband and threw a check at April. "Here's five thousand dollars. GET OUT! We never want to see you again."

With her eyes simmering with hate, April picked up the check and left. "The big, powerful, rich always trample on us downtrodden poor," she muttered as she left.

After April was gone, Jack looked at Carole and asked, "Do you think that was wise, sweetheart?"

"Well," Carole said in her defense, "now she can never again say we haven't helped her. And if she ever comes back and you're not here, I'll call the sheriff."

"Okay, but we have to agree that we never will give her any money again. It was one thing for Dewey to ask for help, but we owe her nothing. Is that understood?"

"Yes, it is," Carole agreed. "I hate to say it, but I'm afraid of her, Jack."

"Well, as soon as she finds another poor sucker like Dewey to get her hooks into, I doubt we'll ever see her again," her husband hoped.

"That would be nice for us," Carole agreed. "But I would feel sorry for whoever the unfortunate man is."

* * *

In Bedford Falls, Peter Bailey, seated at his desk, looked at a letter from his parents. They were standing in front of the Colosseum in Rome. The letter ended with: "Having a wonderful time. Say hello to everyone for us. We love you, and it's a wonderful life." He was still looking at the picture when his two o'clock appointment arrived.

Ben Davies was a securities dealer, and after shaking hands with Pete, he got right to the point. "Mr. Bailey—"

"Call me Pete."

"Like most savings institutions, you probably make about five percent on home loans and pay about four percent on savings accounts with a higher rate on personal loans."

"Yes, that's about right," Pete concurred.

"There are investments that can pay you far more on the capital you have to invest, Pete."

"Let me stop you right there, Ben," Pete said. "My father taught me to avoid risk. Our depositors' money is a sacred trust, and we can't gamble or unnecessarily jeopardize it."

"Your father was a smart man, Pete, and I agree with him one hundred percent," the salesman explained. "But the government has just created an investment called a real estate investment trust, or REIT for short. It is almost as risk-free as what you are doing now. After all, Pete, they're not making any more land."

Pete sat up with interest.

"This is projected to pay ten percent interest at the outset. You won't get that anywhere else without a lot of risks. Also, REITs can be insured."

Mr. Davies was an excellent salesman and shortly, Pete was investing ten thousand dollars in this new investment vehicle. Then the salesman leaned forward and said, "I wouldn't want this to go any further, but I can offer a hot tip for the future." He looked around and said, "There is a local private corporation which I understand will go public shortly."

"Who is it?" Pete asked.

"Cayuga National Corporation. They are putting a lot into fixing their buildings and reorganizing their corporate structure. So, when they go public, it could be really big," Davies explained.

"I've never heard of them," Pete noted with a shrug.

"It used to be called Potter Industries," the man said.

"Potter Industries!" Pete exclaimed. "Henry Potter was my dad's biggest nemesis. A man in here a few weeks ago had a huge check for Dad to make peace. My folks are using it now for a big vacation."

"Well, the previous owner was a miser, who stockpiled cash, and the new management plans to use it to expand and diversify. So, when they go public, I recommend investing in their stock."

"They tried for years to put us out of business," Pete smiled. "It would be ironic for us to now own part of that company and make money on them for a change. What a hoot! Old Man Potter would be rolling in his grave."

"That's the spirit, Pete! I'll let you know the second that stock is available."

They shook hands, and after Davies left, Pete sat down and said, "All those years, Old Man Potter tried to destroy Pop. Now we can own part of Potter's company. Talk about sweet revenge. I love it!"

Chapter Twelve

Jack Curtis's hope for his family to continue as ordinary citizens now quickly disappeared. Each day the mailbox was crammed with appeals from every charity on the face of the earth. If he and Carole went out in public, everyone seemed to be looking in their direction, and Carole complained it was like living in a fish bowl.

Each day Jack cursed the newspaper and its reporter a little more for the story documenting his recent inheritance. The final straw that required them to move from the ranch they loved so much came in late September. The sheriff came by and informed Jack and Carole that three ne'er-do-wells had been planning to kidnap David from the elementary school he attended. Their plan was to collect a half million dollars in ransom. Fortunately, the plot was overheard by others who passed the information along to law enforcement, and it was foiled before they could commit the crime.

As she learned of the planned crime, Carole became hysterical. Jack consoled her as he put his arm around her. "Thank you, Sheriff. We appreciate your diligent work," Jack said.

"You're welcome, Mr. Curtis. I hate to suggest it, but you might invest in additional security, such as a high fence around your home. In addition, we will have a deputy posted to the school for your son's safety."

"We appreciate that, Sheriff. Thanks again."

As the sheriff left, Carole said, "We can't stay here, Jack. We need a more secure location in which to live."

"Yes, I know, Carole. Tomorrow we will go to San Angelo and find a home that's not out in the country. We'll have to live among the more well-to-do folks, who can better advise us on security."

* * *

In Bedford Falls, the Bailey Building and Loan's monthly board meeting was held on the last Friday of the month at six P.M. The news was good and the members were euphoric. Like his father and grandfather before him, Pete did not sit on the board but was available to answer questions and provide suggestions, as the manager, for future projects for which he would gain board approval.

Dave Stevens, who owned the hardware store, was the current board chairman, and as he looked over the financials, he was delighted. "These past five months have been some of the best in our history," he noted.

"Yes, they have been," Terry Brennan agreed. "Pete has continued to serve in the excellent tradition set by his father and grandfather. He is to be commended."

"I move that we give Pete a five percent raise as a reward for his good work," Phil Greer added.

"Before anyone seconds that motion," Pete said, "I would only accept it if it applied to all employees of our building and loan association. I haven't accomplished this alone."

"I now amend my motion to include all employees," board member Greer announced.

Another board member, Janice Redmond, seconded the motion and it passed unanimously.

Shortly after that, the meeting concluded. Pete suggested, "As all of you serve without compensation, I suggest that we meet tomorrow evening, with our spouses at a steakhouse, for dinner paid for by the building and loan."

After additional discussion among the five board members, they agreed upon the suggestion.

* * *

For Jack and Carole, living in the city was a different experience. Now, neighbors' homes were only forty or fifty yards away. Previously, the closest neighbor had been a quarter of a mile down the road. Also, unlike the ranch, where there were chores and taking care of the cattle, there was little to do outside the home in the city. Consequently, Carole became much more involved with the PTA and planned social events for the Cattleman's Association.

Jack could still drive out to the ranch, where he had hired a full-time manager. Finally, however, he began to feel unneeded there. With plenty of money now available, he had purchased the adjoining ranch and more cattle, and his manager was doing an excellent job. It was no longer a hands-on operation for him. But six weeks after moving into the city, an opportunity arose.

At about nine A.M., the phone rang and Jack answered it. "Hello, this is Jack Curtis."

"Mr. Curtis, this is Luther Wendel. I'm the president of Horizon Oil and Exploration here in Midland. I read your interview yesterday in *Texas Business Today*, and I would like to get an appointment to talk to you."

"I can arrange that, Mr. Wendel. What is it you wish to discuss?"

"In your magazine interview, you mentioned your Cayuga National Corporation was looking to diversify. I'm not comfortable discussing business on the phone, but I would like very much for us to meet in person, to discuss a business proposal mutually beneficial to us both."

Immediately, Jack's mind began to consider the situation. He had no fancy office to impress another businessman and was not busy with company matters. However, he did not wish it to look like he had much free time. So, he paused and said, "I can clear my calendar for tomorrow afternoon. How about one o'clock?"

"One it is. I look forward to meeting with you," Luther replied.

"Can you give me a heads-up about what you need to discuss?"

"Yes, I can. I was just hired as the new company president here at Horizon. Everybody said I was crazy to take the job since the owners had run the business into the ground. Still, this can once again become a promising and profitable company with the proper backing." Then he gave Jack a little more background information before Jack asked a question.

"Tell me, Luther, are you married?"

"Yes," Luther replied. "My wife, Megan, and I have three children."

"Well, my wife Carole likes to be involved in my corporate matters. So have your wife come with you, and we can meet in a fine restaurant with a private table. Since it's for business, I will pick up the check."

"Excellent. We'll call you when we get to San Angelo."

After Jack hung up the phone, Carole inquired about the conversation he had just had. "My thrifty husband has offered to buy dinner for another couple. So, what's going on?"

"Call it a hunch, sweetheart," Jack said, "but I think I may have found the answer that I'm looking for."

"Answer to what?" his wife answered.

"I think my company needs to diversify, and I have been racking my brain for a product. With the country investing in highways, I think gas is it. I don't know anything about oil, but this man does. So, I intend to pick his brain for how to go about it. He seems to think a merger with his company is a possibility. So, I'll meet with him and see what he suggests. I can then have the folks back in Bedford falls do the research. It should be interesting if nothing else. But I intend to learn from the meeting."

Carole smiled and said, "What do you think you will learn?"

"I'll find out when we meet," Jack said.

Unknown to Jack at the moment, Luther Wendel was going to provide precisely the solution that Jack wanted for Cayuga National to diversify. The new product was oil.

A Cajun named Francois Hebert had come to the Permian Basin as a wildcatter just twenty years before. He had found success and created a company called The Horizon Oil Company.

Eventually, it was valued at twenty million dollars. When its founder passed away, in 1951, it had one hundred service stations in West Texas and Eastern New Mexico.

Frank (as Francois was known to his friends) left the ownership of his company to his two sons, Claude and Jean, in his will. The two sons were frat boys at Texas A & M University, and used the company as their piggy bank. They threw wild parties and spent ridiculous amounts of time at the Chicken Ranch Brothel in nearby La Grange.

After graduating from college, their conduct did not change. Instead, it worsened as they partied on the Texas Gulf Coast beaches or the slopes at Sun Valley, Idaho.

In the intervening ten years since their father's death, numerous company presidents had resigned in protest over their profligate behavior. Most of the gas stations had closed, and the few that remained open were dirty and unattractive. Now, the boys had hired Luther Wendel as their latest company president. Most of Luther's friends had attempted to dissuade him from the position. But what others saw as a ticket on the Titanic, Luther saw as a diamond in the rough.

After Jean had died in a vehicle accident, Luther decided it was time to convince someone else of the company's possibilities. Now he planned to meet with Jack Curtis.

Chapter Thirteen

After driving into San Angelo, Luther found a parking lot with a pay phone and called the Curtis residence. Jack informed him that he and Carole would quickly meet them where they were.

As they walked outside to the new Buick, Jack commented to his wife, "I sure am glad we bought the new cars. We wouldn't impress anyone with the old Mercury."

"Honey," Carole said, "I think this guy needs to impress you, not the other way around."

"Just the same, sweetheart, it never hurts to act like you're a Rockefeller," Jack said with a laugh. "To tell the truth, it feels nice." As he said that, Carole laughed.

A few minutes later, the four of them were meeting, and after introductions, Carole said, "Honey, why don't you have Luther sit up front with you, and Megan and I can sit in the back."

As they left the parking lot, Jack explained, "We joined the local country club last month, and to tell you the truth, it's taking a little getting used to. I still feel a little out of place when we walk in. However, they promised me a nice, quiet table where we can discuss business without anyone overhearing."

"That's perfect. I think you will like what you hear. If I can get new ownership for Horizon, I think the sky's the limit."

In the back seat, Megan said, "This is a beautiful new car, Carole."

"Thank you," Carole replied. "But, unfortunately, we had to break down and buy new cars as our old vehicles were falling apart."

As they entered the country club dining room, the maître d' nodded and said, "Welcome, Mr. and Mrs. Curtis. We have your table ready."

"Thank you, Stephan. Mr. and Mrs. Wendel will be joining us."

"Excellent, sir! Right this way." He then led the foursome to a table on the far side of the room.

"Where did you go to school, Luther?" Jack asked after they were seated.

"I attended the Forty Acres in Austin. Got my BA and MBA in business management there," Luther said proudly.

"Great, I was a Longhorn, too," Jack replied. "The GI Bill covered most of my time there. After my BA, I got a master's in range management. My thesis was 'Land Preservation and Prevention of Erosion after Range Fires.' Now that I live in the city, I feel like a duck out of water."

Shortly after that, Luther began to give Jack details of the sad history of the Horizon Oil Company and how it had shrunk to a fraction of its previous size. "There are former associates of Frank Hebert who have said they would do business with me, but not as long as his degenerate, unprincipled sons own the company. With one of them now deceased, I think the other might sell quickly."

Jack said very little as Luther continued. "In 1952, Horizon Oil was worth twenty-five million dollars. Today it is worth less than six. I can't spend money on further oil exploration or expansion, as the Hebert boy spends everything on strippers at the Colony Club or the Carousal in Dallas."

"How much do you think they would take to convince the surviving brother to sell, if it were offered to him?" Jack wondered aloud.

"That would depend on whether or not he was sober," Luther replied with a smile. "The company is worth less than six million, so I have no doubt they would take five. But, on the other hand, catch him drunk in a strip club, and he would probably accept less."

"How did you come to work with Horizon, Luther?"

"I learned about the company from a friend of mine. Ben briefly worked for the Hebert Family and told me about their terrible mismanagement. I researched and accepted the job as their company president because if I could find new ownership, I could build that business back into a top-tier oil company. If not, I would resign like the previous man did. I then took the job as their company president over my wife's objections because I could see the possibilities."

"Could you be more specific?"

"There are some assets Claude doesn't know about," Luther said with a smile. "With proper management, that company can take off and be profitable beyond anyone's imagination."

"Tell me more."

After their wives excused themselves to go to the ladies' room, Luther lowered his voice. "The Hebert Brothers did some illegalities a while back and framed the friend I previously mentioned, Ben Hartwell, for the actions. It's because of conduct like that, that nobody will work with them."

"Then why did you take the job?" Jack inquired.

"Because of the information Ben gave me."

"And what was that?"

"Ben had an ace in the hole for me to use for revenge," Luther smiled. "Horizon owns an oil lease on the northern coast of Papua New Guinea. The Hebert boys were unaware of it. After what Claude and Jean did by framing Ben for their activities, he kept the knowledge to himself. Six months ago, it was discovered that the coast of New Guinea was awash in oil. If I can acquire new company ownership, I can get some revenge for my friend and have a great position in a profitable oil company. That's why I took the job everyone warned me to stay away from."

"That's very interesting," Jack agreed.

As Jack listened, Luther continued. "If the current owner knew this information, it would just be more money for him to use, indulging in more debauchery and depravity, and the company would eventually be bankrupted. After what they did to Ben, I figure withholding the information is the punishment Claude has coming. It's revenge for doing harm to a very good man. Besides, with new ownership, I would be able to hire more people and run a profitable company for the benefit of everyone."

Jack sat for a moment. He was unsure about the legality of withholding information from an employer, and the action's morality was definitely questionable. Luther was stabbing his current owner in the back, but if he were as corrupt as Luther suggested, maybe Claude deserved it.

Luther continued. "All I have to do is drill on that leased section, and Horizon will be extremely profitable. You would increase the net worth and profitability of Cayuga National immensely, if you acquired Horizon Oil."

"Let me run things past our mergers and acquisitions people and get back to you," Jack replied. "I don't dare mention the part about withholding information from the current owners, but if things are as you say, I think we have a deal."

"How long do you think it will take to complete the purchase?" Luther asked.

Jack smiled and replied, "That will depend on how hard Claude Hebert negotiates. I don't want him to think it is important to me. I want him to think I'm doing him a favor."

The two couples enjoyed a relaxed dinner and afterward went to Jack and Carole's new home. "We're still getting settled in," Carole said as they showed the Wendels their new house.

"I think it will be beautiful when you get it the way you want it," Megan commented.

"I hated to move from the country into the city, but we needed to improve our home security situation," Carole explained.

After returning the Wendels to their car, Carole asked, "How did it go, honey?"

As Jack detailed his conversation with Luther, Carole had one question. "If he is willing to stab his current bosses in the back, can you trust him to work for you?"

"He was up front and honest with me about his actions. However, I would keep a cautious eye on him. But if everything is as he says it is, it is a deal I would be crazy to pass up. In the meantime, he seems mostly anxious to gain some revenge for his friend. I can understand that."

"Well, do what you think is best."

Chapter Fourteen

Jack got the long-distance operator on the phone and had her put through a call to Harvey's office in Bedford Falls. After one ring, Harvey answered.

"Harvey, who do we have taking care of mergers and acquisitions?" Jack quickly asked.

There was a pause, and Harvey answered, "No one currently."

"Well, appoint someone. I don't want to conduct business on the phone since I don't know who might be listening, so I will be in town Tuesday. I have some ideas I need to run by everybody. I will fly into the Bedford Falls airport, and you can have a limo pick me up there."

"No problem, Jack. Will you be staying for the directors' meeting on Friday?" Harvey asked.

"Yes, I will. I have read some good things in the trade papers. So, I need to give you people a pat on the back."

"Great! We'll see you then."

Meanwhile, Phil Gallagher had received a background report he had ordered from the Erie Investigative Services. He was meeting with four of the other board members. "According to this report, Jack Curtis is a Boy Scout. He is so squeaky-clean; it's scary," Gallagher reported.

"What does it say?" Tim Murrey asked.

"He was 82nd Airborne during the war. Numerous decorations, including two purple hearts. Master's degree from University of Texas, model citizen . . ."

"You mean he didn't go to a real school!" Ethel Thomasson snorted.

"The rest of the country would tell you Texas is a real school," Murrey responded.

"Not like the schools we attended. I went to Bryn Mawr," Ethel replied. "Places like Texas just play football."

"Well, he is definitely not a rube or a hayseed," Murrey noted.

"Maybe, he will be good for the company. The fact that he didn't sell to us shows he is interested in the long term and wants to make money," McClusky added.

As Ethel continued complaining, Murrey said, "You're just mad because Potter didn't leave the company to you."

"Well, yes. I did Potter's dirty work for twenty years, and he as much as promised he would leave it to me."

"Stand in line, Ethel," Gallagher responded. "He made me the same promise. But really, when did Henry Potter ever keep his word about anything?"

After a few profanities about her former boss, Ethel muttered, "At least you wound up with some stock from the old buzzard."

* * *

Jack's plane landed at Bedford Falls Airport at nine-thirty A.M. As he stepped off the plane, he wasn't ready for the cold New York weather and the freezing north wind. Fortunately, chauffeur Tom Munson was waiting for him. As Tom opened the limo door, Jack said, "Thanks, Tom, I appreciate your work. It was sixty-five degrees when I left home this morning in Texas."

"Welcome back, sir. I'm sorry it's only twenty degrees here."

"It's not your fault," Jack joked. "You're not the weatherman."

The first stop was to be the accounting firm of Porter, Morgan, and Price, but Jack had his driver stop first at a department store to get a warmer coat than the light jacket he was wearing.

Shortly after that, as he met with one of the accounting firm's partners, he realized his life was becoming more complicated. The accountant, Richard Porter, informed him that the income tax rate for over two hundred thousand dollars of income was ninety-one percent. After Jack almost choked, his CPA told him that the trust was structured, so most of the revenue was capital gains taxed at only twenty-five percent.

"My gosh!" Jack commented. "Uncle Sam sure wants his share. After I sold my cattle last year, I paid less than two thousand dollars in taxes, and this year I'll pay over sixty times that amount."

Mr. Porter laughed. "Believe it or not, this country was founded so our citizens would not have personal taxation."

Jack shook his head at the bad news and joked, "Withhold enough money from the last trust payment of the year to keep the government happy, and I'll let my wife know we're not as well off as she thought."

The next stop for Jack was the company headquarters, where he was running his ideas past Harvey. Meeting with them was the newly hired vice president of mergers and acquisitions, Terry Zikus.

"There is an oil company we can get for bottom dollar," Jack said. "I'm not at liberty to tell all I know, but it should be worth over a hundred million dollars in ten years. We can get it for about five percent of that amount currently."

"What is the name of the company?" Terry asked.

"Horizon Oil," Jack replied. "It has been mismanaged and is now almost bankrupt. All you need to do is spread the word that we want to diversify into the oil business. Pretend to have several companies you are looking at, but are mostly interested in Horizon due to the possible low cost. Bluff 'em that you are doing them a favor."

Terry Zikus smiled. "Sounds like you have some inside information, sir."

"I prefer to call it what a good infantry recon team would call intelligence before combat," Jack replied.

"After we acquire this company, who would you want to run it for us?" Harvey asked.

"Their current president, Luther Wendel, is a local man with an MBA from the U of T and knows the oil business. In the negotiations, agree to keep all current employees at their jobs. Suggest that is because we expect everyone to work harder for us than they did the former owners."

"Jack," Harvey smiled, "why do I suspect you have more than your arm up your sleeve?"

"A good poker player never shows all of his cards until he has what he wants," Jack replied with a grin. "Let's just say I might have a few aces."

"Mr. Curtis?" Zikus asked quizzically.

"Call me Jack. There's no need to be so formal."

"New York City recently held its annual toy show. A new toy company was trying to get off the ground, and no one was interested. However, with the baby boom occurring since the war, we could make a fortune if we acquired them and properly financed them. Of course, everybody else thinks I'm crazy, but I think it could be a gold mine."

"Do it! You have my permission."

"Are you sure about that, Jack?" Harvey asked.

"Harvey, my kids are always looking for the newest toy. If we advertise on Saturday morning television, I don't think we can lose," Jack explained. "Of course, everything would have to be planned around a big push toward next Christmas. If it doesn't work, you and Terry can blame me."

"I'll hold you to that," Harvey laughed.

At one o'clock, Jack was present for the monthly board meeting. It was routine, and Jack was surprised there was little opposition to the suggestion that Cayuga Nation diversify. The only ones who seemed to take a genuine interest in the meeting were Jeff and Mayor O'Reilly. The other four were unusually silent. Jack wondered what was on their minds. Then after he gave his last suggestion, they seemed more excited.

The suggestion was, "I would like us to take this company public next September after the new acquisitions have proven successful."

"Excellent!" Exclaimed Gallagher. "Our company attorneys can prepare the voluminous paperwork and with the amount of treasury stock we have available, we don't need an underwriter. Normally before an IPO you issue stock and find an underwriter to oversee the process. Between our attorneys and our bank, we can eliminate much of the red tape. It's nine months until next September, which gives us more than enough time."

As a move toward that goal was made and seconded, Jack wondered about their sudden enthusiasm and interest.

Before returning to Texas, Jack paid another visit to George and Mary Bailey. Their son Pete and his wife Pamela were also there. The four were looking at photographs of the trip to Europe George and Mary had made some months previously.

As Jack arrived, George shook his hand vigorously. "Jack, I want to thank you again from the bottom of my heart. I always told people that Uncle Billy never took that money. Thank you for proving me right."

As Jack continued to shake hands with everyone, Pete said, "A securities broker mentioned a rumor you were going public soon and recommended we buy the second the stock is available. He expected it might do well in the future."

"Yes," Jack agreed. "We plan to make the move next September. I believe that if you purchase our stock, you will be very pleased with the result."

"Well, I'll be doggoned," George interjected. "I never dreamed the building and loan might ever make money on Potter Industries."

"The name is Cayuga National, George," Jack reminded him. "Potter Industries no longer exists."

"Oh, oh, that's right," George hesitated. "I forgot there for a minute. I remember talking to Clarence fifteen years ago—" Pete cut him off.

"Dad, I don't think Jack wants to hear any angel stories today."

"Son, I swear to you that event happened," George insisted.

Before anything further was said, Jack said, "I would love to hear the story. My mother always insisted that angels occasionally help people."

A half an hour later, Jack was leaving after hearing the story of how an angel named Clarence Odbody had saved George's life in 1945. As Jack departed in the limousine, Mary said to George, "It's such a wonderful life, everything should always go perfectly for us from now on."

Mary had no idea just how wrong that prediction would be. There is an old adage that says, "If you think your life is perfect, you have overlooked something."

Chapter Fifteen

April Curtis was performing at Jack Ruby's Carousel Club in Dallas when Claude Hebert walked in. Total nudity in a public business was against the law in Texas, so the female performers were required to wear the minimum attire allowed by the current legal code. However, the employees were allowed to perform privately for large tippers in a private room, where no one asked questions afterward. April provided Claude Hebert with such an individual performance.

April always could attract men she assumed had money. Unfortunately, she had misjudged her late husband. Dewey Curtis had inherited a cattle ranch from his father. However, it was half of the spread his father had owned, with the other half owned by his brother. Dewey walked with a cane and was not a good businessman. In addition, April milked him for everything he was worth until he passed away from a stroke. Her brother-in-law bought the insolvent ranch and refused to assist her farther financially. Now she seethed with anger to the point she could almost foam at the mouth.

As Claude gave April an additional one-hundred-dollar tip, April said. "Oh, thank you. You are so kind, but I must go home and get something to eat. I've been working since early afternoon."

"Well then," Claude answered, "there's a restaurant down the street. Why don't you join me for a late dinner?"

"You are just so kind," April purred. "Why, thank you. That would be much better than a peanut butter sandwich at home."

"Peanut butter!" Claude exclaimed. "Is that all you are looking forward to?"

With her most pitiful look, April answered, "Times are not good and sometimes money is tight."

"Alright then," Claude commented. "Let's go eat."

As they got into Claude's new sports car, April knew she had picked the right man. "I can tell you are a successful businessman. So, what is it that you do to improve the world for the rest of us?" she asked.

"A year ago, I sold my oil interests for four point nine million dollars," he explained.

"That's incredible. You are clearly a brilliant and successful man."

"Well, maybe not," Claude said sadly. "Right after I sold, some of the foreign leases produced big time, and the company was worth ten times that. So, I would be better off today if I held on to that business."

"That's so sad," April consoled him. "Who did you sell to?"

"Some outfit back east in New York, I never heard of, called Cayuga National."

"Cayuga National!" April screamed. "That's the company owned by my scumbag ex-brother-in-law. I bet that crook cheated you."

* * *

Where There Is Life There Is Always Hope

The school year would start soon, so Jack brought the entire family to New York to end the children's summer vacation. David would be in the second grade in two weeks, and Liz would begin kindergarten. Carole was looking forward to days with no children home until the afternoon. Jack would attend the monthly board meeting to tie up loose ends before the IPO, and the family could tour locations in New England and the Central Atlantic area.

As the meeting began, most items were mundane until they discussed the upcoming IPO. Jeff went over the details. "While we legally don't need an underwriter, the recent acquisitions have made our company much more valuable. Therefore, to ensure our stock is priced correctly before the upcoming action, we have brought in an investment bank to provide that oversight."

Mr. Gallagher asked, "What number have they come up with as an initial stock price?"

"They divided the current value of the corporation by the two million shares that were available since Potter founded the company, and came up with a price of thirty dollars a share," Jeff explained.

"Then, to lower the price and make it more attractive to all investors, I move we do a two-for-one stock split before the IPO," Gallagher said.

After a little more discussion, the motion passed unanimously.

* * *

One month later, with the proper paperwork filed with the government; Cayuga National stock was available to the public. With his previous heads-up from a friendly broker as well as Jack Curtis, Pete Bailey invested twenty thousand dollars in Cayuga stock. By day's end, the stock's worth had tripled to over sixty-one thousand dollars. However, Pete was angry that he had not invested more aggressively with building and loan funds. He slammed his fist on his desk, mad that he had not purchased more stock. He swore that in the future he would be more willing to accept more risk with his business investments.

* * *

Meanwhile, Jack informed his wife that their net worth had increased by over sixty-one million dollars during the day following the IPO. At first, Carole sat in shock. Then, she said, "Honey, think of all the wonderful things we can do with that money." She started to list ideas when Jack interrupted.

"Sweetheart, we don't have the money. It is simply an increase in the worth of our stock. To get the money, we would need to sell some of the stock," he explained.

"Why would that be a problem?" she asked.

"Well, we would have to pay twenty-five percent capital gains taxes."

"That leaves us with three-quarters of the money. I think we can get by on that," Carole reasoned.

Jack took a breath and calmly explained, "Carole, I have heard of people who gained a windfall of money and quickly spent it, and wound up as poor as they were in the beginning. I grew up poor and refuse to let that happen to us. I never want to be poor again."

"You're not the only one," Carole argued. "During the Depression, I always had holes in my shoes. I had to put cardboard in them and always had wet feet when it rained. So, let's use our money to help others."

"Then we will have freeloaders like April coming out of the woodwork demanding we give them money. I don't want that to happen," Jack countered.

"Forget April!" Carole shouted. "We've helped her enough. If we gave her everything we have, it still wouldn't be enough. I'm talking about people who could actually use some help."

"How do we tell the difference?" Jack demanded.

"We will have to find a way. But, Jack, some good people need help, and we can't be greedy and selfish and ignore them."

"Okay," Jack agreed. "But I do not intend to go bankrupt helping them." With that exchange, the argument ended as Jack hugged his wife, knowing the subject was bound to resurface later.

Chapter Sixteen

It was July 1963, and Jack met with Luther in Midland. The news was fantastic. In the almost three years since Cayuga National had purchased Horizon Oil, the company's value had increased from less than five million dollars to nearly two hundred million. As they talked, Luther's secretary informed him he had a visitor from Washington.

Luther sat up straight in his chair, and his face lost all color as he answered, "Yes, Margaret, show the man in."

Jack sat silently as a large man in a dark navy-blue suit walked into the room. He showed an FBI badge and said with a big smile, "I am agent Philmont from the Dallas field office." He held out his right hand.

Luther immediately rose from his chair and shook the man's hand. He quickly pointed to Jack and introduced him as well. After shaking Jack's hand, the FBI agent got to the point. "Claude Hebert has lodged a complaint with the SEC that he was somehow defrauded in a conspiracy between yourself and Cayuga National Corporation. He cites evidence that his company increased in worth by four thousand percent immediately after being sold to the new owner."

"I can reassure you that there is no validity to that statement," Luther said, trying to sound confident.

"I have no doubt that will be the case, as the vice president has briefed me on this matter," the agent agreed.

"Tell the vice president his confidence in us is well founded," Luther replied.

"Thank you, Mr. Wendel." The agent turned to leave and then stopped and added. "By the way, certain individuals would consider it a personal favor if you would not extend your company's reach and your franchisees into the southeast and coastal part of the state."

Knowing powerful people did not want the competition, Luther smiled and agreed. "Consider it done, Agent Philmont. We have no intentions of expanding in that direction," Luther agreed with a big grin.

After Philmont left, Jack exclaimed, "What was that all about? The area between Austin and the gulf coast is the most lucrative part of the state. So, why would you agree not to expand there?"

Luther replied. "What do you know about Vice President Johnson, Jack?"

"I've heard you don't want to piss him off. You never introduce your wife to him unless you remain by her side, and he's as treacherous as a snake," was Jack's reply.

"You just insulted snakes, Jack," Luther replied. "Johnson is so crooked, they will have to screw him into the ground when he dies. Some people have wound up dead when they got in his way. I don't intend to be one of them. But I'll honor his wishes if he doesn't want us competing with one of his friends."

"I've heard he can be a sleazy character," Jack agreed.

"That's the way he works. A friend who has done him a favor wants something, so he then promises to help you in return.

Maybe having Claude Hebert's complaint go away is worth it," Luther explained.

Jack studied Luther's scared demeanor for a second and said, "Well, expanding into Oklahoma, New Mexico, and Kansas should be profitable."

"Thanks, Jack. I was hoping you'd see it that way," Luther replied.

* * *

On November 21, 1963, Jack and his family were visiting Bedford Falls. George Bailey and his wife Mary had invited them to join their family's Thanksgiving celebration. There were sixteen people present. The spouses of Pete and Jane were there, along with their four grandchildren. Susan and Tom were still unmarried, and tolerated their parents' suggestions that they look for eligible singles to whom they could tie their respective nuptial knots.

Upon arrival, George asked them, "What are you people up to these days?"

Carole looked proudly at Jack and said, "You tell them, honey."

Jack then explained that Carole had argued for almost a year that they were duty-bound to help others with the means that fortune had blessed them with. "I finally conceded and set up the Curtis-Taylor Benevolent Trust," Jack explained. "I have endowed it with a grant of ten million dollars to assist others who are in unfortunate circumstances."

"That is so cool," Susan exclaimed. "I wish other rich people would do such good deeds."

"Zuzu gets excited by that bleeding heart stuff," her brother Tom said with a roll of his eyes.

"The name is Susan," she replied. "Zuzu was my childhood nickname."

"Tell them the best part, honey," Carole insisted, ignoring Susan and Tom.

"My wife here is the CEO and administrator of the trust," Jack said. "She has set her yearly salary at two dollars. That way, she makes twice what I make as the board chairman at Cayuga."

After everyone congratulated Carole on her new role, it was a pleasant day. There was no further discussion of business as the two families enjoyed the celebration. Nine-year-old David was quieter than usual, spending most of the day with Pete's eight-year-old daughter Emma.

* * *

The next day was the monthly board meeting at Cayuga. It had been postponed a week due to a significant snowstorm the previous Friday. At one in the afternoon, Jack called the board meeting to order. Everything was routine. The upcoming tax cut the president had submitted to Congress and its effect on business was the main item of discussion, and business was excellent.

Then an hour later, a secretary entered from the adjoining office with tears in her eyes. "I'm sorry to bother you, Mr. Curtis, but there is news on the radio I think you need to hear."

Turning in his chair, Jack said, "Turn up the volume."

Then everyone in the meeting heard Walter Cronkite's words, "It is official. President Kennedy was pronounced dead.

He was shot thirty minutes ago, and doctors have just made the announcement. We now take you to a reporter on the scene."

There was total shock in the room. Even Ethel had tears in her eyes. Jack immediately said, "I will entertain a motion to adjourn." The meeting quickly ended as everyone present considered the tragedy. Several were wiping their eyes as Jack said, "Lyndon Johnson is now president."

"Is that good or bad?" Harvey asked.

"I don't know," Jack replied. "I guess only time will tell. One thing for sure, he is in a position to quell all the investigations into his questionable business conduct."

Chapter Seventeen

Carole Curtis sat at the desk in her home office. She had a picture of her family behind her desk and a large calendar on the wall to the left. It was March 2, 1967, and as she considered other changes of décor, she pondered how life had changed. Seven years ago, Carole had no money to buy new clothes and drove a car more than ten years old. She and her husband had to decide which bills to pay and which to put off until the next month. Now they were among the wealthiest people in the Trans-Pecos area. They had even hired a housekeeper and gardener to take care of mundane dusting and cleaning and yard work.

The charity Carole administered had been a learning experience. First, she had to learn to discern between those with temporary needs and freeloaders, to whom no amount of help would ever be enough. Sadly, she had discovered her former sister-in-law, April was not the only human leech sucking the blood of society. However, there were others who had a temporary need and, after receiving help, would honestly try to repay the kindness to help others.

After the charity had been established, Jack had a contractor add a side door to the house so those with business could come to the office without knocking on the front door. It was precisely ten A.M. when Zuzu Bailey came in the door. Her hip-hugging bell-bottom jeans and loose-fitting peasant blouse were in stark contrast to Carole's business attire. Likewise, the ribbons and flowers in her hair informed all that she was part of a different generation.

"Good morning, Carole. Where do you want me to begin?" Zuzu said as she greeted Carole.

"There is correspondence that needs to be typed and sent out in the daily mail. So, you should start with that."

As Zuzu sat at the typewriter, she inserted a sheet of paper and started to type. "Oh, you're not donating to the Humane Friends of Wildlife?" she asked.

"That's right," Carole said firmly. "We discovered their entire budget goes to overhead. They don't give a single penny to the cause for which they are collecting."

"You're kidding!" Zuzu replied.

"No, I'm not," Carole explained. "The couple that runs the so-called charity pays themselves a six-figure income, and the rest of the money they collect goes to advertising. I have a letter to the Internal Revenue Service requesting they end the charity's nonprofit status."

"I'll type that one first," the young lady decided.

Carole set aside the stack of requests for help she was analyzing and said, "I need to compliment you. You are prompt, reliable, and dependable, and I appreciate that."

"Thank you, Carole. And thank you for hiring me. I enjoy this so much better than the frumpy old college I was attending off and on."

"I never had the chance to attend a college and wished I had," Carole noted.

Later, Carole asked a different question. "When I first met you, you insisted your name was Susan. Now you prefer to be called by your youthful nickname. Why the change?"

"It's more unconventional. Everyone wants to be the same in today's society, and I think I need to be an individual. Dad said he gave me that nickname because, as a toddler, that's how I pronounced my name. I can't think of anything more cool or original than naming myself. I gave it up at college because others thought it was stupid. However, I finally decided I liked it."

"I don't think there is anything wrong with being an individual," Carole replied. "If you like it, then that's what you need to do."

"I have a question," Zuzu asked. "For over twenty years, my family had heard how an angel saved Dad's life when Old Man Potter tried to have him arrested. But others derided the idea when I told the story to them when I got older. The typical reply was, 'Your old man got drunk and imagined the whole thing.' Some people acted pretty nastily." Then with a pensive look, she added, "What do you think?"

"I know things happen in this world that no one can explain. Impossible things happen, but there are witnesses. So, if the result of something inexplicable is positive, then I tend to believe the story. If the result is otherwise, I get more cynical. However, your father is alive, and the story ended well, so I would give him the benefit of the doubt. Who cares what others think."

"Thank you, Carole. I'll remember that." Then, after typing for a while, Zuzu commented, "After work tomorrow, I'll be going to Houston. They're having a big anti-war rally."

"Please don't mention that to Jack," Carole commented. "He has no use for the anti-war movement."

* * *

In Bedford Falls, Pete had been working on the business expansion for some time. Now he had a much larger building, along with two new locations. With the changes, however, he needed a name change. So, Pete had suggested, and the board approved, the name of Central New York State Savings and Loan Association. With the new locations in surrounding cities, the money was rolling in, and now the association could make loans for much bigger projects.

George dropped in to see his son in the main office. "What do you think, Dad?" He said as he showed George around the new building.

"The purpose of a building and loan was to make loans to individuals traditional banks overlooked. You might be getting in over your head, son," George suggested.

"Dad, the economy is booming, the opportunity is here to do bigger and better things, and I think we should take advantage of it. They say opportunity only knocks once," Pete explained.

"Opportunity can knock any number of times. So, it is best to make sure you pick the right ones." George continued to have reservations about the direction Pete was taking the business. "Pete, I was there for years to welcome the owner at every home or business built with one of our mortgages. Are you able to provide that personal touch now?"

"The business is way too big today for that, Dad. This is 1968, and things are done differently," Pete explained.

"Maybe you're right, son. But it would be best if you never lost the personal touch. It's what makes people believe in you and trust you."

Where There Is Life There Is Always Hope

* * *

Jack and Carole had just eaten at a Mexican restaurant on a visit to Arizona. The food was good, and he thought it might be what he was seeking. So, he talked to the owner. His name was Oscar Vasquez.

"Have you ever thought of franchising the business you have here?" Jack said as they shook hands.

"That would be nice, but I have my hands full with this location," Oscar replied.

"I can help with that," Jack said. "If we could come to an agreement, Cayuga would provide the financial backing while you oversaw the individual restaurant franchises."

Finally, Oscar said, "Let me think about it."

Jack had thought Cayuga National was ready to expand into another industry. He had noticed how hamburger eateries were opening up everywhere, and he believed that a fast-food franchise might be an excellent addition for Cayuga in the future. So, he carefully planned his pitch to the board in the event Oscar agreed. It would not be just another of the hamburger joints starting to dot the countryside, but something new, and Oscar's theme and décor were perfect.

Unfortunately, he would also suggest to the board the possibility of opening new corporate headquarters in Texas, which would meet with opposition and play into the hands of his enemies.

Chapter Eighteen

Jack was making fewer and fewer decisions for Cayuga National. Harvey had complained that Jack was making too many decisions without consulting him first. When he mentioned it to Carole, to his surprise she agreed with Harvey.

"Honey, Harvey is the company president. It should be his place to make all these decisions."

"But, sweetheart—" Jack argued.

"You're micromanaging the company, Jack. I'm surprised Harvey hasn't complained before," Carole explained.

To end the argument Jack agreed not to call Cayuga on mundane matters and let Harvey do his job. Then, Jack received a very unusual telephone call. Jeff Cooper was on the line and sounded concerned. "Jack, our stock is doing extremely well. It's risen over nine and a half points over the past week."

"That's a good thing, isn't it?" Jack replied.

"Normally, I would say yes," Jeff agreed.

"Then what's the problem?"

"Our stock price has risen steadily the past two years, but it usually has been a point or so every few months. We haven't made any public statements to gain public interest. It's very unusual for something like this to come out of the blue," Jeff replied.

"Well, let's sit back and wait and see what happens."

"We will be monitoring the situation. But, in the meantime, I figured I should let you know," Jeff said.

"Thanks for the heads-up. In the meantime, I'm sure Harvey can handle everything."

"Who was that, honey?" Carole asked.

"It was Jeff. Cayuga stock is doing so well, maybe I shouldn't have sold so much of it these past two years," Jack replied.

"Well, selling the stock allowed you to buy the real estate you acquired, and it endowed the Curtis-Taylor charity your wonderful wife administers, giving us a great tax deduction," Carole said with a smile as she kissed him. "Besides, you still own almost a quarter of Cayuga National. I'm sure you're still making plenty of money."

"Yes, the real estate I bought is still worth more than the stock I sold. I'm sure it's nothing to worry about."

However, Harvey, Jeff and other company officials continued to notice the stock price rise at an unusually rapid rate. Jack assumed that was a good thing.

* * *

Unbeknownst to Jack and most Cayuga officials, sinister events were taking place. These involved Claude Hebert and a member of the Cayuga Board. The two had met some three months before the unusual rise in the stock price. It had been April who gave Claude the initial idea.

When April first met Claude Hebert, she saw him as her next meal ticket. However, she quickly discovered her first impression of him was incorrect. While he at first appeared to be a former partying frat boy whose pockets she could easily pick, she quickly found that was inaccurate. This fellow had brains.

After selling his company To Cayuga National in 1963, Claude Hebert reinvented himself. He realized the money he received from the sale wouldn't last forever with his extravagant lifestyle. So, he looked around for another way to make money.

As a consultant, he would advise companies not doing well to buy up smaller businesses. They could divert assets they needed and sell assets they didn't. Claude would realize an excellent payday for his actions, and the only losers were those laid off from the acquired company. The process worked so well that Claude could not imagine why no one had thought of it before this time.

It was 1967, and Claude and April were enjoying a few days at the Horseshoe Casino in Las Vegas. After a winning evening at the blackjack table, they were enjoying a romp in the bedroom when April suggested, "Why don't you go after my ex-brother in-law's business next? He deserves it."

"That's a pretty big company, April. The process would take a lot longer than normal."

April laughed. "Taking longer would make for a bigger payday," she suggested.

Claude mulled over that thought. "You know. I think you're right. When we check out of here, let's go to New York."

After Claude contacted Rochester International Manufacturing, they quickly hired him as a consultant after verifying his reputation in his line of work. Claude immediately traveled to the Bedford Falls area to begin his new project. His investigation revealed that board member Phil Gallagher was ambitious and had expressed anguish that Potter had not left Potter Industries to him. He met Phil in a bar on the outskirts of Bedford falls.

As they met, Claude introduced himself and suggested he could help Phil become the chairman of Cayuga National. Being cautious, Phil said he would think about it, and they should meet again in five days. Phil then had an investigator check into Claude's work and kept the appointment, as they met less than a week later.

"Mr. Hebert, it's good to meet you. My friends at the SEC tell me you've been complaining about my company," Phil said.

"Call me Claude, and it's nothing personal. My grudge is against Jack Curtis. That man has cheated me out of millions."

"Tell me about it. I find that very interesting," Phil said.

Claude gave a long, sad story about how his oil company had terrible luck during the economic recession of the late Fifties, and the company's value had plummeted. However, its value increased by over four thousand percent immediately after selling the business. It had to be more than a coincidence. He suspected that someone had withheld valuable information from him.

"Well, Claude, you came to the right man. Our founder promised me control of this company, but he double-crossed me and left it to someone he had never met. We offered Curtis a more than fair price for his share of the company, and the greedy jerk turned us down."

"I can help you gain control of Cayuga National, Mr. Gallagher," Claude quickly said.

After another drink, Phil laid his cards on the table. "You have quite the reputation, Mr. Hebert. If I did things your way, they would gut my company, and I'm sure I would wind up unemployed. However, I have a better idea." As Claude tried to interrupt, Phil said, "Hear me out."

"Okay," Claude answered.

"You begin the way you have planned. That is, begin the anonymous trading in a name that Cayuga personnel cannot trace to Rochester Corporation. You will have my assistance and when we reach the magic number, make it appear that I double-crossed you and took control. You would have your pay from Rochester, and I would pay you double that amount. I would then have my company intact, and we would not harm the economy of my hometown. The only losers would be Rochester, but you're from Texas. Why would you care about them?"

With a big grin, Claude said, "I think we have a deal. I like teamwork. Do you have any information that will help me in this quest?"

"Yes," Gallagher smiled as he explained the situation. "Jack Curtis has done a lot of profit taking to invest in real estate and be a philanthropist. He no longer owns a majority interest in this company."

"You don't say!"

With a big grin, Gallagher said, "He barely owns a quarter interest in Cayuga National now. Fortunately, he's not a local, so I suggest we acquire a majority interest, vote him out of the chairman position, and take over the company."

"Well, let's get to work," Claude eagerly said.

Phil reached over to shake hands and said, *"Enchante de faire votreconnaissance."*

Claude was shocked. "You speak *francais*."

"Yes," Phil responded. "And as a Cajun, I figured you also did, as well."

"Well, so no one else knows what we're saying; let's stick to that language in the future, when we talk business," Claude said with a smile.

"Oui, c'estce que nous allons faire," Phil replied as they shook hands.

Claude's extensive investigating had paid off, and he found a willing conspirator to participate in a hostile takeover of Cayuga

National. He would have to double-cross his original friends in Rochester, but that didn't bother him at all. He would make a lot more money this way.

* * *

In Bedford Falls as the anonymous trading began, Phil was very discreet. Not knowing who might work with him, he went first to Mayor Patrick O'Reilly. "Pat, we've noticed a larger-than-normal movement in our stock. But, of course, you wouldn't know anything about it, would you?"

The mayor shrugged. "No, but if sales are strong, that's a good thing, isn't it?"

"Usually, yes. However, I wondered if one of those big corporate giants in the Big Apple might be trying to move in and take over."

"If they are, we need to stop it!" Mayor O'Reilly angrily snapped. "Jack Curtis is the best thing that ever happened to this town. The unemployment rate here is almost zero, and business is great."

"I agree," Phil said with a deceptive smile. "I don't think we have anything to worry about. Although, maybe I'm a little paranoid since things are going so well. So, forget I said anything."

"Okay, Phil, but let me know if you find anything funny going on."

"Will do," Phil said as he scratched Pat off his list of helpers.

Ethel Thomasson was more accommodating. She had been forced to retire a few months after Jack took over, but she was allowed to stay on the board so her monthly stipend from board service could supplement her social security and small monthly Potter Industries pension. She agreed with Phil.

In the last election, Bill McClusky was upset by a younger, more youthful candidate. Even though Jack had given him a sizable campaign donation, he felt it was not enough. He blamed Jack for his defeat. "Old Man Potter wouldn't have let me loose," was his lament. He told Phil, "If we can take over and you become board chairman, I want to be company president."

"The job is yours," Phil said with a handshake.

Tim Murrey was more ambivalent. "Things have been great since Jack Curtis has been here. So why would we vote him out?" Tim asked.

"Well," Gallagher replied, "you could become company president unless you want to be in the state senate forever."

Senator Murrey thought for a few seconds and replied, "I won't stop you. If you can pull it off, you have my blessings if you'll agree to my being company president."

"Then we have a deal," Phil said as he shook Tim's hand. The duplicity of his conduct didn't bother him at all, since he figured the end justified the means.

Phil Gallagher did not talk to Jeff Cooper about his plans. He knew Jeff often played Golf with Jack when the latter was in town. So, Phil would quit while he was ahead. He would also make sure Harvey McClellan was out of the loop. Harvey and Jack were as thick as thieves. He had to smile at that analogy. After all, he and his friend Claude better fit the definition of crooks.

The two conspirators persuaded friends to purchase Cayuga stock. In addition, board members had stock options they could exercise without raising suspicion. So, the group continued to buy stock for the next couple of months. Everyone was instructed to explain that it was a good buy and that they followed a hot tip. After all, many financial workers said they recommended Cayuga National as an excellent buy.

Chapter Nineteen

When you live in San Angelo, Texas, and the headquarters of the corporation for which you are the chairman of the board is over seventeen hundred miles away, life isn't always easy. Jack considered travel in the corporate airplane too expensive to use as the only passenger. Even if he took his family along, it was still prohibitively expensive. It was cheaper to have the family fly with the public. Since he did not want his children to think they were in a privileged class above others that was another reason to fly commercial.

Of course, the trip to Bedford Falls always included a visit with George and Mary Bailey. Carole had hired their daughter to assist in her charity work, and Zuzu was an excellent worker when she wasn't participating in an anti-war rally. Having fought in Europe during the last world war, Jack disliked the peace movement. He saw the push by others to disarm our country in the face of enemies as insanity. However, Carole seemed to get along well with Zuzu. Therefore, he kept his ideas to himself to have peace in the family.

One thing to be thankful for was that Cayuga National Industries was not a defense contractor. As a result, there were no protests around its corporate headquarters. Jack and his family could fly into town and visit with their friends, and Jack could attend his meeting with little conflict. He could also smile at the puppy love that was budding between fifteen-year-old David and Pete's daughter Emma. While there was strife and turmoil on the nightly news, Jack was confronting no problems—or, so he thought.

As he and Jeff met with Harvey in his office, there was concern voiced by the other two men.

"Someone is buying up our stock," Jeff said. "It's mostly anonymous trading, so we have hired a private investigating firm to discover what it is all about."

Jack was intrigued. "Were they able to get to the bottom of it and discover what's going on?"

"Yes, they did," Harvey replied. "Rochester International Manufacturing is attempting to acquire us. Unfortunately, their stock price and profits are down, and they see getting ownership of us as an excellent way to improve their company. Since Potter died, we have had exponential increases in sales and profits, and they are like a hungry kid looking at a chocolate cake."

"If there was a merger, how would that affect us?" Jack inquired.

"They would loot many of our assets to improve themselves. And there could be layoffs here in Bedford Falls," Jeff explained.

"Then we can't let it happen," Jack defiantly announced.

"Sadly, that's not all, Jack," Jeff added. "There's more you need to know."

Taken aback, Jack asked, "Oh, what else is there?"

"According to the investigators, the enemy has inside help from someone within our company," Harvey explained. "It would make sense that it's someone on our board."

* * *

Later, before the monthly board meeting began, Jack was friendly and shook hands with everyone. However, he kept his demeanor as always, careful not to show undue concern. As the meeting began, Ethel read the minutes from the previous month.

There were no additions or corrections, and the minutes were quickly accepted as read.

Then a review of the financial statements showed nothing but positive data. Several board members voiced their delight, and Jack said, "Do we have a motion to accept the financial paperwork as presented?"

"It's good news, the same as always," Phil Gallagher noted. "I move we accept the balance sheet, income statement, and cash flow statement as presented."

"Second the motion," Mayor O'Reilly said.

The motion passed unanimously, and Jack got into other business. "Our Horizon Oil subsidiary has just spun off another subsidiary. It's called The Horizon Chemical Company. Our auditing firm will travel to Midland for the quarterly audits to ensure everything is in order. So, I'll be flying back in our company plane with them."

Then pretending he had a lapse in memory, he paused and said, "Oh, I probably should have mentioned this before, but I'm sure it's nothing." Then with his eyes carefully looking straight ahead to observe the others seated around the table, he casually said, "We've received a report that Rochester Manufacturing is desirous of merging with us." Jack noticed Phil Gallagher brought his hand up to his chin as he said that. He then said, "We are currently more profitable, and I see no reason to consider such a move. However, if anyone has any thoughts, I would be happy to hear them."

"Located on Lake Ontario, they have a large shipping division. So, perhaps, we should look into it," Phil smiled.

Jack then asked for other thoughts and, hearing none said, "I'll have Harvey look into it, and if anyone has further input, they can provide it to him."

He then changed the subject. "With so much of our business being in the West, I wondered if maybe we shouldn't set up a secondary or satellite headquarters in Texas. I think that eventually, technology will be like Dick Tracy, where we will have telephones where we can see who we're talking to and secure phone lines where you can talk without outsiders listening to the conversation. It could cut travel costs and provide better communications for our operations."

"Are you planning to move the company headquarters to Texas," Phil asked?

"Not at this time. Bedford Falls will always be the national headquarters. But as we continue to grow, our subsidiaries may want a more central location to work with. On the other hand, with improved technology, this one location we have now might be more than sufficient. It's just something to think about. Either way, the final decision would have to be a board decision."

Jack would come to regret the suggestion he had just made.

Chapter Twenty

After the meeting, Jack met with Jeff and Harvey in the latter's office. "I'm guessing the person working with Rochester is probably Phil," Jack suggested. "You better keep an eye on him."

"I agree," Harvey concurred. "But I think we need to be looking around for others in case he might not be the rat in the nest. And if he is, he may not be alone in this matter."

Jeff Cooper changed the subject. "Are you considering moving the company headquarters to Texas, Jack?"

"No! We're incorporated in New York State, and moving would involve more problems and red tape than I want to consider. It was just a brainstorming idea since Texas has no corporate income tax, but I think it could create more difficulties than it would solve. So, it needs to be discarded. So, you can forget that idea, because I have."

"Good. Talk like that might make some board members nervous, let alone stockholders," Jeff replied.

* * *

Phil Gallagher met with Claude Hebert, speaking French. Phil reported that Jack had suggested moving company headquarters to Texas, and Claude quickly decided they should spread that rumor to all stockholders, and company employees. That was a good strategy, but their idea of conducting their conversations in French was less so, since speaking in French in an upstate New York bar could draw the attention of others.

April Curtis was not the patient type. Claude had explained that they needed to bide their time and relax. That was a plan she resented, and she was starting to spend time drinking in the local bar where Claude worked secretly with some of the locals.

One late afternoon she visited the bar where she planned to meet Claude and began to drink. After she had started enjoying her third martini, the bartender casually asked, "Why's an attractive lady like you sitting all alone? I'm sure plenty of fellows here would like to buy you a drink and provide you with some company."

Unfortunately for April, too much alcohol made her a little too talkative. "As soon as my husband finishes his business, he will give me all the attention I need. I'll have him and a lot of money when we blow this town. That will be all I need," she said as she took another sip.

"What business is your husband in?" the bartender casually asked.

"Let's just say he redistributes wealth," April cryptically replied. Then with a sneer, she added, "And he takes a nice piece of the action in return."

"Sounds like an interesting job. But who is he redistributing wealth from?"

"Nobody you'd know," April replied. "Just a worthless scumbag named Jack Curtis."

The bartender perked up at the mention of Jack's name. Like many others in Bedford Falls, he knew the name as the man who had replaced Old Man Potter and had drastically improved the city. At that time, the bartender had to tend to two men who had walked into the establishment and ordered beers, so he poured two on-tap beers for them. One was Phil Gallagher. The other sat next to the lady who cheerfully greeted him. It was the man he had seen the day before speaking French with Phil.

Bar owner Harold Baxley came out of the back office to change the drawers in the till for a shift change. Noticing Phil, he greeted him. "Hi Phil, long time no see. Who's your friend?"

"I'm Claude Hebert. I'm a tourist from France and met Phil here who's showing me around. It has been good to find someone who speaks my mother tongue," Claude explained.

"Where did you learn French, Phil?" Harry asked. "I didn't know you could speak it."

"My first wife was from France. I met her during the war and learned the language from her. I haven't had a chance to use it for some time and Claude's giving me a chance to brush up on it."

Harry shook hands with the two of them and said, "Good seeing you, Phil. I hope Claude has a great time here in Bedford Falls." However he wondered what the purpose of speaking French with Phil was. What was it that they didn't want others to understand? However he had things to do, so he picked up the drawer with the day's receipts received so far, which he placed in the safe and left for home.

April left her seat to go to the powder room as the bartender brought the beers over. "Here you go, guys," he said. "Is there anything else I can get for you?"

"No, but I need to pay my girlfriend's tab, as we need to leave shortly," Claude said.

The bartender collected the money and said with a laugh, "She told everyone else to leave her alone because she was waiting for her husband."

In a low voice, the man shook his head and commented, "We're not married, but she calls me her husband. You know how women are."

"I understand, pal," the bartender answered. He put the money in the till, and shortly afterward the three people departed. Still, he made a mental note about the episode. Something about Phil's friends seemed unusual.

* * *

The next day, Phil met with Bill McClusky. "In a couple of months, we should have everything all lined up where we can take over."

"I'm looking forward to it," Bill said. "We vote you in as board chairman, and I will be the new company president. That is the deal, right?"

"Correct!" Phil said as they shook hands. Phil smiled as he considered he had made the same deal with Tim Murrey. He would worry about that later.

* * *

Meanwhile Jack took the time to visit George and Mary Bailey and share some of his concerns. "Your word carries a lot of weight in this town, George, and I need your help," he began.

"What can I do for you?" George replied.

"Rochester International Manufacturing is attempting to get control of Cayuga and, apparently, someone on our board is helping them. If they can get control, I'm sure it won't be good for this city. They would strip away the most profitable sectors of the company, and right now, that's our oil interests, and sell off everything else. As a result, there would most likely be layoffs in Bedford Falls."

As George listened, he was horrified. "How can I help you?"

"Start spreading the news to anyone who owns Cayuga stock that any change in corporate ownership could be disastrous."

Mary smiled, "George bought some shares a year ago. He thought it would be poetic justice to be a shareholder in Potter's old company."

"What little we own won't help much, Mary," George replied. "Jack needs bigger shareholders than us to accomplish what he has to do."

"Every little bit helps," Jack countered. "Even one share gives someone voting rights. You need to convince any friends or neighbors who own Cayuga stock to hold on to them. Whoever wants to buy is probably someone wanting to dismantle the company. We need all the help you can provide."

"You can count on us," George assured.

"If anyone says the offer they got is too tempting to pass up, tell them I will match it," Jack emphasized. "We need to ensure the company leadership remains in local hands."

Chapter Twenty-One

Harvey and Jack went to see Pete at the savings and loan as it opened for the day. They explained their concern about the move by Phil on behalf of the Rochester Corporation.

"That could be disastrous for Bedford Falls," Pete agreed.

"Yes," Harvey said. "That's why if you hear of anyone desiring to sell and feel it is too good of a deal to pass up, Jack will meet the offer they have."

Harvey nodded as Jack said, "That is correct."

"Some people have been told there is a chance the company may move to Texas, and folks around here might have to move or be unemployed. They seem scared," Pete explained.

"That is a lie," Jack immediately said. "I only suggested moving the company offices, but even that is off the table. The factories were never in danger of moving, let alone being closed. Everyone's job is secure."

"I'm happy to hear that," Pete agreed. "I'll ensure as many people get the word as possible."

That same morning, Harry stopped at the bar. He retrieved the money placed in the safe the night before and drove to the savings and loan to deposit the funds. Harry noticed Harvey and Jack as he walked into the building and walked over to say hello.

"Hi, Harvey," Harry said, shaking hands. "You should come over to my place as much as Phil does. We could use the business."

"You've been seeing a lot of Phil lately?" Harvey asked.

"Yes, he's been meeting with some red-haired French tourist." They speak French but I don't know why, since the guy speaks real good English."

Jack looked stunned as he asked, "He had red hair and spoke French?"

"Yeah, Larry said a week ago, he spoke good American English. He was with some bleach-blond, who had her black roots showing."

"That sounds like Claude Hebert and my former sister-in-law, April. If they are together, that's real trouble for us."

"Sounds like you know them," Harvey commented.

"Yes, obviously, they're the ones causing us problems. We need to stop next at Bedford Falls National Bank and give Phil his walking papers. He is clearly in cahoots with them."

With a big smile, Harvey said, "Well, let's get into the limo and make a necessary trip." Then to Harry, he said, "Thanks, Harry. You answered a lot of questions we've been wondering about." After that, Jack and Harv left the savings and loan and headed to the bank.

After stopping at the bank, the two men walked through the revolving door and stopped at the office of assistant manager Steve Harwell. The door was open, so Harvey looked in and said, "Steve, can we see you in Phil's office for a moment?"

"Sure thing," he replied and joined the two men.

The three walked to Phil's office. The door was closed, but Harvey opened it and said, "You're fired, Phil! Don't bother cleaning out your desk. We'll have someone do it and send you your stuff. Just get out of here! Steve is the new bank manager."

While Steve was utterly shocked, Phil sat straight up in his chair and stoically said, "Fine, I'll go. But the yearly meeting is in three days, and when it's over, we'll send Jack's cowboy butt back to Texas, and you can update your resume." With that, he stood up and, without a word, left the bank.

Harvey turned to Steve and said, "Congratulations, your promotion is effective immediately." He and Jack then shook his hand.

As they walked out of the bank, Harvey said, "That was fun. Now let's make sure we have our ducks in a row."

After leaving the bank, Phil Gallagher went to a phone booth and called Bill McClusky. His first words to his fellow conspirator were, "They're on to us, Bill. They just humiliated me in front of my employees."

"How much do they know?" Bill asked.

"I don't know. But it doesn't matter if we've counted our votes correctly. In three days, we can send that Texas clown and his lackey down the road."

Chapter Twenty-Two

By Phil Gallagher's count, he had at least fifty-five percent of the stockholders lined up on his side. Tomorrow he would take control of Cayuga National Industries and become board chairman. It had been a long, hard battle, but the end was in sight. He had stayed at home and bided his time for the past two days. Jack Curtis and Harvey McClellan had humiliated him in the bank he had managed for twenty years, and he was determined to repay them in kind.

Meanwhile, as Phil was averse to being seen in public, Bill made the rounds dealing with those he knew agreed with them. He made sure their support was solid.

With the state senate in recess, Tim Murrey was at his insurance office, and Bill paid him a visit. Tim had him come into his office and shut the door.

"How are things going, Bill?" he asked.

"Couldn't be better, Tim. After tomorrow, this company will be entirely under local control by us Bedford Falls citizens."

"Once that is taken care of, what changes does Phil plan for the corporate structure?" Tim asked.

"Well, obviously, Phil will be the new board chairman, and he promised me the job of company president."

Learning that Phil had promised the company presidency to another, as well as himself made his blood boil. However, Tim kept his poker face saying, "He's got things planned that far, has he?"

"Yes, and you can pick whatever position you want in the company after that," Bill explained.

Tim forced a smile and said, "All we have to do is count the votes."

"That's right," Bill said. "Well, I have to run. There are others whose support I need to confirm."

"I'll see you guys tomorrow," Tim said as he sat back down. Then in his mind, Tim said a plethora of obscenities to describe Phil Gallagher. *I always knew that jerk's word was not worth what's on the bottom of a bird cage*, he thought. He smiled. *Thankfully, Bill McClusky has a big mouth and an empty brain. It's no wonder he lost the last election. Like Phil, he lied to too many people.* He looked around and considered. *This time Phil lied to one too many.*

As he considered his options, he figured it best not to tip his hand that he was aware of Phil and Bill's untrustworthiness. Tomorrow, something might change. If it did, he would be sure to get any promises in writing.

* * *

Jack, Harvey, and Jeff Cooper visited Pete Bailey after the savings and loan closed at five o'clock. Pete had them come into his office, and they carefully considered the situation.

"I've been talking to everyone and even got Dad involved," Pete explained. "So many people are scared of the company leaving town. I was afraid they might not believe me, but Dad had dealt with them for over forty years. I assured him the company is staying put in Bedford Falls, and he gave his word to everybody." Pete looked to Jack for assurance of that fact.

"Pete, I can swear on a Bible if you wish. Cayuga National is staying here in Bedford falls," Jack stated.

"That won't be necessary," Pete replied. "How are things looking for tomorrow?"

"It's hard to say," Jeff replied. "It could go either way, but it looks like we don't have the votes. I hate to admit it, but Phil might be the winner tomorrow."

"We will meet in the city hall auditorium," Harvey said, explaining the details. "Our company auditors will verify each voter and the number of shares. I guess we will have to hope for the best."

"We can do better than that," Jack said. "I checked with our lawyers, and according to them, we can require anyone who wishes to speak to fill out a paper which tells their name, with a summary of their comments, and I get to determine the sequence of the speakers." Jack emphasized that fact. "How do you think I should handle the order of speakers?"

After a few seconds, Jeff had a suggestion. "You go first, Jack. Then we'll hear from those who want change. Then, lastly, all those who wish to keep the company leadership as it is presently. I think our supporters should go last to have the final word."

"Dad owns a few shares," Pete spoke up. "Have him speak last of all. If he can't win everyone over, no one can."

"Then, that's what we will do," Jack said. "If we're all in agreement, let's call it a day and pray for the best."

Jack went back to his hotel room and called Carole. He told her of the developments in Bedford Falls and that he was depressed.

"Honey," she replied, "if you get voted out of control of the company, there is no limit to your options. With all the real estate you've bought, you can become a real estate broker, or go back to ranching. Best of all, you won't have to go out of town so much. The kids miss you when you're gone. Sometimes I wish you would step down as board chairman, anyway."

"I know, Carole, but I have so many plans about how to enlarge and improve this company," he replied.

"Honey," she said softly, "how much did you say we were worth when you were home the other day?"

"Over two hundred and fifteen million dollars," he admitted.

"Seriously, Jack, that's already more money than we can spend in our lifetimes. How much more do you think we need?"

"I guess I just don't like to lose," he replied.

"Honey," Carole told him, "to me and the kids, you will always be a winner. Don't worry about that vote tomorrow. I don't think it is that big of a deal."

After telling Carole good-bye he hung up the phone and wished he could be as ambivalent about the situation as she was.

Chapter Twenty-Three

It was Friday, September 27, and it was raining as Jack looked out the window of his hotel suite. *It's just as well*, he thought. It was a dreary, miserable, wet day that would go well with his despondency. As he checked his tie and appearance in the mirror, he thought, *Time to go get voted out*. He wished so badly that he had paid more attention to the events of the past eight months. Then he tried to think positively. He wasn't like Louis XIV. That guy lost his head. Jack was only losing the position of Cayuga National board chairman. It only paid him a dollar a year (as well as occasional use of the corporate airplane and the best hotel suite when he was in town). But, he realized, worst of all, it would hurt his pride.

As Harvey and Jeff arrived in the limo, he walked out of the hotel. The chauffeur opened the door for him.

"Thanks, Tom," he said as he got in.

"You're welcome, sir," the chauffeur replied. "Sorry about the weather."

"At least we're on the green side of the grass. It could be worse," Jack noted.

As he got in, Harvey said, "I guess we get to see Phil take over the company today. I'm sure he won't do as well as we have. He'll be more like Henry Potter."

"If we get voted out, let's go out with our heads held high," Jack replied. "I think we've done a whale of a job and nothing to be apologetic about."

Upon arriving at the city hall, the three men went inside, where everything was being set up. Outside the auditorium, as one entered the building, were three tables where stockholders checked in and had their voting status verified. If they were also voting for other individuals, they were required to have proxy forms signed by those persons. Also, anyone who wished to speak was given a speech note on which they wrote their name and a summary of their speech. Finally, each stockholder received copies of the current audited financial statements and an invitation to the luncheon following the meeting.

On the other side of the doors entering the auditorium were two additional tables which displayed coffee urns and donuts for those attending. Over the entrance to the auditorium was a large banner that announced Welcome Stockholders and Friends of Cayuga National Corporation.

Up front on the podium were nine chairs for Harvey, Jack, Jeff, and the other six board members. The first ten rows in the audience were reserved for stockholders, with the remaining rows for the press and other observers. In addition to the microphone on the podium, two others were used by audience members.

Jack walked over to the table with the coffee and got himself a cup. As he did, Tim Murrey came over and said, "Good luck, Jack," as he extended his hand.

As they shook hands, Tim slipped Jack a note. Jack said, "Thank you, Tim," and put the message in his pocket. He then walked toward the men's room to be alone. Once inside, he quickly unfolded the piece of paper. The note read, *Me and my seven percent of the stock are with you. Good luck, Jack.*

It was enough to make him smile. Jack assumed four board members opposed him, but it was only three. Things were looking up. Now he figured the odds of success were close to even.

At nine, Jack called the meeting to order. "If everyone will please stand, patrol leader Paul Collingsworth from our local Boy Scout troop will lead us in the pledge of allegiance to our flag," he instructed.

After the audience recited the pledge, Jack introduced those sitting on the podium. He asked for a round of applause for their service. Then he continued with the perfunctory agenda meeting items. Ethel read the minutes from the meeting held the year before, and then it was time for comments from the audience. Jeff had sorted the speech notes into two stacks representing pro and con opinions and gave them to Jack.

"We will now entertain concerns from the audience. In the interest of time, we ask that you hold your statements to three minutes. Mrs. Thomasson will be our timekeeper, and she will stand up at two minutes and forty-five seconds, and when she sits down at three minutes, we need everyone to thank our speaker with a round of applause."

For the next hour and a half, people rose to praise or complain about some item. Some were like the woman who wailed, "I'm worried the company might move to Texas, and my husband will be out of work after all these years."

Jack assured her there were no plans for such an event. While Texas had no corporate income tax, there were other fees that dictated that such a move would be unwise. He stated the woman had nothing to worry about. Cayuga would not relocate to Texas. However, it was disappointing that others continued to express the same concern. As those seeking change in company leadership finished speaking, there was applause.

Then others stated opposing thoughts. One example was, "Eight years ago, stores were closing in Bedford Falls, and young people were leaving after high school and not returning. That is not happening anymore, and with the assurances, we have received that our factories will continue to remain here in perpetuity, we will continue to grow and prosper."

George Bailey finally gave his impassioned, short speech at eleven-fifteen. Jack watched the audience, looking for how George's words were received. People were attentive, but he could not ascertain how it might affect their vote. At the conclusion of these speeches, the applause was almost identical to these approving of the previous speeches. Jack was nervous. He had no idea how the result of the voting would go.

Jack kept his poker face and asked for a motion to end the speeches. After being moved and seconded, a vote was taken on the motion, which passed overwhelmingly. It was time to elect the new corporate chairman of the board.

Harvey then rose and said, "I nominate Jack Curtis as the chairman of the board of Cayuga National."

"Second the nomination," said Jeff Cooper

Bill McClusky then nominated Phil Gallagher, and Ethel seconded the nomination. Finally, a friend of Phil rose and said, "I move nominations cease."

It was quickly seconded, and after a vote passing the motion, the stockholders went to the tables where the company auditors tabulated who had voted, the number of shares they controlled, and who they voted for. The votes that had been phoned in by stockholders unable to attend the meeting were also added. Unfortunately, no one would know the results until after lunch.

Harvey walked over and said, "It's been good working with you, Jack. I hate to see things change."

Jack smiled, pulled the piece of paper from his pocket to show Harvey, and said, "I think the result will be closer than we thought. Tim gave me this before the meeting began."

"Well, I'll be danged!" Harvey said. "I had no idea he was with us."

"That makes two of us," Jack laughed. "Now, let's go talk to Phil and his friends."

They walked over to the other board members talking near the podium, and Jack extended his hand to Phil. "If you win, Phil, I will ask our stockholders and friends to support you one hundred percent," he said with a big smile.

"Well, thank you, Jack. And I will do the same for you."

"Also, Phil, if I win, I will be announcing the retirement of you, Bill, and Ethel from the board. I would recommend you not try to fight against that announcement."

Phil stiffened his back and frowned. "Fine, if you win, we will accept that," he defiantly said.

As Jack and Harvey walked away, Phil huffed and said, "Do you believe the nerve of that guy, thinking he is going to win?"

"That was perfect, Jack," Harvey said. "You got them to agree to walk away quietly or wind up looking like fools. I just hope George Bailey's little speech did the trick."

"As, do I," Jack sighed. "Let's find Jeff and go get some lunch. No use sweating it out on an empty stomach."

The votes weren't tabulated and verified until shortly after one. Then, as the meeting reconvened, the chief auditor read the elections final result. There was complete silence as he started to announce the result. "Stockholders and friends of Cayuga National Corporation, it was very close, but we have the final tabulation of the votes."

Phil Gallagher was beginning to stand and be recognized as the auditor said, "With fifty-three-point one percent of the vote, the chairman remains Jack Curtis." As people started to applaud, an embarrassed Phil sat back down.

Jack returned to the rostrum and announced, "During the lunch break, three long-serving board members notified me of their need to retire from our board and we need to replace them today. But first, please give thanks and a big round of applause for Phil Gallagher, Bill McClusky, and Ethel Thomasson for their long-time service." The three individuals sheepishly stood to acknowledge the applause.

Toward the end of the meeting, Jeff, Tim, and Pat had been reelected, and the stockholders elected other board members to join them. They were David Thayne, who owned an automobile dealership; Brian Jacobson, who was principal of the high school; and sixty-one-year-old George Bailey, who was one of the most respected men in Bedford Falls.

Chapter Twenty-Four

Phil Gallagher was not a happy man. Like all low-life individuals, he blamed others when anything went wrong. He was convinced Claude Hebert had made a mistake that had tipped off Jack to the conspiracy to take over Cayuga National. He had paid Claude twenty thousand dollars for his assistance in the recent plan and had nothing to show for it.

Now, Phil called the president of Rochester International Manufacturing, Rollo Brinkerhoff. "Mr. Brinkerhoff?"

"Yes, who is this?"

"I'm Phil Gallagher, a member of the board at Cayuga National here in Bedford Falls," Phil explained.

"What, may I do for you, Mr. Gallagher?"

"Some time ago you hired Claude Hebert to assist you in a takeover of my company," Phil explained.

"I have no idea what you're talking about," Mr. Gallagher. "Now, if you'll excuse me, I have work to do."

"Don't hang up, Rollo," you'll find this interesting.

"In what way Mr. Gallagher?" an exasperated Brinkerhoff asked.

"Well, when we met, Hebert made me a deal that if I paid him twenty thousand dollars, I could take over the company. That way he would get paid twice. Unfortunately, he messed up the entire deal and you and I are both out our money. I just wanted someone else to know that I wasn't the only one cheated on the deal," Phil explained.

"I have no idea what you're talking about, Mr. Gallagher. Good-bye." With that he hung up the phone.

Quickly Rollo called a business agent at the local Longshoreman's Union. Dino Lombardi took the call. "This is Dino," he said, as he answered.

"Dino, this is Rollo, I need some help cleaning up some debris at a site."

"No problem, meet me at the Southside Bar at five-thirty and we can work out the details." Dino smiled as he hung up the phone. "That man always provides plenty of work," he said quietly to himself.

As they met at the bar, Rollo explained the situation. "I hired a guy named Hebert to do a job a while back and he double-crossed me. He promised to do the same job for someone else so he could get paid twice. I need someone to take ten thousand dollars out of his hide."

"The usual fee?" Dino asked.

"Yes," Rollo replied. "A thousand dollars up front. Don't kill him. Just make sure he thinks twice before he pulls this stunt again. He is staying at the Northern Lights Motel in Bedford Falls." He then handed Dino a Rochester Manufacturing check for one thousand dollars. The memo line on the check said site cleanup work.

Dino then paid two men four hundred dollars each to go to Bedford Falls and complete the job. Before the two men arrived, Claude had asked April to go down to the motel office to buy some cigarettes. She had no money in her purse, so grabbed his wallet, which was sitting on the dresser and walked down to the office to make the purchase. As she was returning, the men arrived and began to beat Claude within an inch of his life. As she looked into the room, Claude was screaming and she was horrified at the brutality of the beating. She panicked and jumped in his car and took off with his wallet, which had two hundred dollars and his credit cards.

When Claude woke up in the hospital, he had a broken jaw, four broken ribs, a broken arm and a hairline fracture of his tibia, among other injuries. When he learned April had run out on him, he reported her for car theft and credit card fraud (she had charged over three hundred dollars in her flight). The car theft charges would be dropped, but April was convicted of credit card fraud and sentenced to a year in jail. She was paroled after six months.

When she was released from the Bedford Hills Correctional Facility for Women, she called Carole. "Carole, its April and I need help."

Carole sighed and said, "What is it now, April?"

"My boyfriend framed me for credit card fraud and sent me to jail here in New York. I just got out and I need help," Carole sobbed.

April was crying so much, Carole almost felt sorry for her. "What is it you want, April?" Carole asked.

Jack was overhearing the conversation and asked, "What's wrong with April now?"

"She just got out of jail in New York," Carole replied, as she put her hand over the phone.

Jack busted out laughing, "That's a good place for her. She'll get free room and board from the state. She should love that."

"She says she was framed," Carole added.

"Sweetheart, you and I both know she's guilty as sin of whatever crime she was convicted."

"Honey, she is really crying. She sounds sincere."

"Carole, give me a break. You know April's never been sincere of anything in her life except her desire to hurt everybody else." He hesitated and said, "You do what you want."

"April," Carole said into the phone.

"Yes?"

"I'll wire two hundred dollars to Western Union first thing in the morning. After that, you're on your own," Carole explained.

"Oh, thank you, Carole. God bless you," April said.

"You're welcome," Carole replied.

"I hope you know what you're doing," Jack said.

"Honey," Carole replied. "I'm sitting on a ten-million-dollar charitable trust. I think I can give two hundred dollars away."

"Even to April?" Jack exclaimed.

"Yes, honey, even to April."

* * *

A couple of months later, Jack was reading the newspaper as his son asked a question.

"Dad?" sixteen-year-old David inquired. "The Central Texas father and son fishing tournament is coming up. Let's enter it."

"That's the week of the Cayuga board meeting, son. I don't think I can," Jack replied.

"Okay, Dad," his son said and disappointedly walked away.

"Jack, can I talk to you?" Carole asked.

"Yes, sweetheart, what do you need?"

Carole looked at her husband and quietly said, "You need to miss the meeting and take your son fishing."

Jack was perplexed. "Carole, that board meeting is important. There are a lot of important things to be discussed. There are

discussions of expanding the company into other fields of business."

"Seriously, honey, Harvey is more than capable of taking care
of all that. You admit he is always available and can advise the
board on all needed actions."

Jack shook his head. "Honey, every move the company makes
increases our net worth. I need to be there to ensure things are
done right."

Carole laughed. "What is our net worth today, Jack?"

He took a second to think and replied, "Today we're worth
roughly two hundred and fifty million dollars. You know that."

"Yes," Carole replied. "We have two hundred and fifty million
dollars and only one son. You need to spend time with him and
let Harvey do his job. I'm sure he can do it quite well, without
you."

"But, Carole—" he began to argue.

"Jack," she said raising her voice, "did your father ever spend
much time with you as you were growing up?"

"No. He had to work at least two jobs to pay mom's medical
bills and put food on the table. Besides, it was the Depression. He
taught me to work."

"I bet he wished he could have spent time with you, Jack."

"Maybe so. He died in a work accident while I was gone in
the war. Mom died about a year later. I didn't even get a chance
to go to attend their funerals," he said with tears in his eyes.

"Well, we have all the money we will ever need and we have
a son who needs to spend time with his father. Now do it," she
demanded.

"Fine," Jack relented. "If it means that much to you, I'll
do it."

Carole stood up and put her arms around Jack. "It'll mean a lot more to you and him," she said as she kissed him.

"Call Harvey or George and tell them I will have to miss the meeting, honey. I gotta go and help David get our fishing tackle ready."

Carole then called both Harvey, who was the company president, and George Bailey, who was now vice chairman of the Cayuga board, to explain why Jack would miss the meeting. Both of them agreed with her that it was a good idea.

Chapter Twenty-Five

It was July 3, 1973, and Carole was on the civic committee that planned the Fourth of July celebration. This year she was planning to make it one that people would remember for a long time. The meeting ended as finishing touches had been arranged for the rodeo, the grand parade, and the fireworks display. Jack entered the room and approached Carole with a melancholy countenance.

"I just got a call from Pete," he said.

"Is anything wrong?" Carole asked.

Jack frowned. "George had another heart attack. He's passed away. Zuzu's taking it badly. She was close to her dad."

"When is the funeral?"

"On Saturday. I already told Pete we would be there," Jack explained.

"Honey," Carole replied, "I think we should go the day after tomorrow. But, first, we must let everyone know we will be out of town for a few days."

Jack smiled and replied. "Also, you want to see the result of all your good work."

With a demure smile, Carole admitted, "That too."

Where There Is Life There Is Always Hope

* * *

After the plane landed and the Curtis Family had walked out of the terminal in Bedford Falls, chauffeur Tom Munson was there to meet them. As he opened the door, he said, "Welcome back, Mr. Curtis. I wish it were a happier occasion."

"As do I, Tom. This city has lost a great man," Jack commented.

After everyone was in the car, Tom took his place at the wheel, lowered the barrier behind them, and asked, "Mr. Curtis, would you like the paper?"

"Yes, thank you, Tom," he said as he reached for the newspaper.

Jack opened to the obituaries and began to read what was said about George. His mortuary tribute covered almost the entire page. At the end of the obituary, he read, "Survived by his wife Mary Hatch Bailey of Bedford Falls; sons Peter Jackson Bailey II (Pamela) of Bedford Falls and Thomas Frederick Bailey (Kathy) of Long Island; daughters Janice Bailey Radzinski (Fred) of Cleveland, Ohio, and Susan Bailey Davis of San Angelo, Texas; and eight grandchildren."

"They have me as Davis!" Zuzu protested. "I've been divorced from that jerk for over two years."

"You'll have to talk to whoever wrote this," Jack laughed. "But if this is the worst thing that will happen in your life, things should be great from now on."

"I hope so," Zuzu said. "Being called by my worthless ex-husband's name is bad enough. I want to forget that bum."

As they walked into the hotel, Jack was about to get rooms when the desk clerk said, "Welcome, Mr. and Mrs. Curtis. The executive suite has been reserved for you." He handed Jack the key.

127

"Wow," Jack said. "Being an emeritus board chairman has its perks."

Once in the room, Carole called Mary to express her condolences.

"Thank you, Carole," Mary said. "With his family's history of heart trouble, it shouldn't have been a shock, but it is, and I'll miss him. However, I'll get through it with my family and friends."

"Zuzu is anxious to see you," Carole replied. "Jack will rent a car, and we'll bring her over."

"Nonsense," Mary said. "I'll have Pete come get all of you. I would love to visit with you."

Shortly afterward, Pete arrived. He put Zuzu's suitcase in the trunk, and the five got into Pete's Pontiac to proceed to the Bailey residence, where she would spend the days before the funeral with her mother.

There were hugs and a few tears, and after visiting for a while, everyone went to the mortuary. Several extended family members were there, including Pete's daughter Emma. David gave her a handkerchief to blot her tears as he consoled her. George lay in repose in a dark blue suit. As they observed him, Zuzu began to cry. Carole put her arm around her.

"After you resigned as board chairman, Dad was elected the new chairman. He was so proud to be the chairman of the board of Potter's old company," Pete said to Jack. "These last three years were some of the happiest he said he ever had."

"I'm glad I could make it possible, Pete. I definitely had other things to take care of, so he was welcome to the position."

At the mortuary, Mary stood by the coffin. Jack came over and said, "I think we all need to get something to eat, Mary. Please join us."

With tears in her eyes, she replied, "I don't want to leave."

Carole said, "The rest of your family needs you, Mary. Please join us. Besides, you better accept when my cheap husband offers to buy dinner for everyone. It might not happen again for a long time."

"Thank you, Carole," she said. Everyone then went to a restaurant. The cars were a little crowded, so David was happy to have Emma sit on his lap.

* * *

The funeral was scheduled to be held in the only facility in town capable of holding the expected crowd, the high school gymnasium. Mourners were allowed to pay their respects from five to ten P.M. on Thursday and Friday and from eight A.M. to noon on Saturday, when the service was to begin. Hundreds filed by the coffin Thursday and Friday as George lay in state in the gymnasium. There were times when the line to enter stretched around the block.

Mary insisted on being there to thank those who came, and Zuzu remained with her mother most of the time. If Zuzu left, her sister or brothers supported their mother. Many mourners had tears in their eyes as they passed. The scene was in stark contrast to the funeral of Henry Potter about twelve years before. Many businesses posted a notice on their door Saturday morning which said, "Closed in memory of George Bailey." It almost looked like people were honoring a beloved international leader instead of a humble local citizen. The Right Reverend Morgan presided over the funeral, and Pete gave his father's eulogy as many wept.

The day before the funeral, Pete had asked Jack to say a few words, and Jack attempted to decline. Finally, Pete replied, "Dad respected you more than anyone else he had ever met. Please do it, Jack."

Jack humbly replied, "It will be an honor, Pete."

So, toward the end of the service, Jack stood at the microphone and said, "I only knew George Bailey for twelve years, but that time has been one of the high points of my life. If everyone on earth lived like George, the world would be a much better place. George was a friend to all and did no ill to anyone. So, as we say good-bye today, let's all try to follow his example and strive to improve the world for the betterment of all. I believe that is the only thing George would ask of us. Thank you for allowing me to remember my friend."

The family followed the hearse in the mortuary limo, and company officials followed them in a chauffeur-driven company limo. Jack declined to ride with them, and he and his family followed in a rented car. Much of the city's population followed the funeral procession as Bedford Falls experienced the end of an era.

Chapter Twenty-Six

It was 1976, and the United States was celebrating its bicentennial. However, that was not the only reason the Curtis family was in Bedford Falls. While Jack wanted his son to be a Texas Longhorn, like himself, David had chosen to attend Columbia University. His reason was not that the school was a prestigious Ivy League institution. Instead, he decided on Columbia because Emma was attending Barnard College in the exact location in New York City.

"Why is it that a man must always follow the woman wherever she is before they get married?" Jack wondered.

"It's only fair since she usually has to live in his shadow after they get married," Carole mused.

"Sweetheart, when have you had to live in my shadow?" Jack inquired with a confused look.

"Well, let's see," she began. "First, I became Carole Curtis and had to learn to ranch, and then—"

Jack interrupted, "Sweetheart, I thought you had enjoyed our life together."

"Oh, I've loved our life together. It has been wonderful. But you must admit that I have always been considered number two by our society," Carole explained with a smile.

"Well," Jack said with a laugh, "Every good trail boss needs a good ramrod, and every great football coach needs excellent assistants. You should be happy, as I decided to have you as my only assistant."

Carole playfully elbowed him. "You would have been in divorce court if you tried to have more than one."

At that point, David came out of the dressing room to show off his tux. "Well, how do I look?" he asked.

With a smirk, Jack said, "Like a waiter at a fancy restaurant."

"He does not," Carole said with irritation. "He looks like he's getting married."

"And he is almost as handsome a groom as I was twenty-three years ago," Jack mused.

"You were not wearing formal attire when we went to the Baptist Church twenty-three years ago, honey," Carole corrected. "He is much more handsome."

Later as their daughter Liz was trying on her bridesmaid dress, she talked to her mother.

"Emma is so beautiful; it almost makes me want to get married. But I'm scared," she said. "I always wonder if a guy who asks me out likes me or is trying to have access to my family's money."

"You must use your best judgment and follow your heart simultaneously, sweetie," her mother said.

"It's hard, Mom. It is. A lot of the rich boys are spoiled brats. One of their mothers even had the nerve to call me a nouveau riche social climber. I wanted to slap her, and I couldn't stand her son. Sometimes I wish I had been born poor."

Carole laughed. "If you spent as much time as I did picking cotton during the Depression, you wouldn't say that. But, I promise you, having money is much better. It just gives you a different set of problems."

The following day at eleven o'clock, the wedding began. As the minister said, "John David Curtis, Junior, do you take Emma Marie Bailey as your wife . . . ?" Carole's memory went back to the day she and Jack were married. Times were much better now, and Carole said a silent prayer that David and Emma would be as happy as she and Jack were.

After the wedding, there was a luncheon at a fancy restaurant for over two hundred friends who attended the wedding. Then at six P.M., there was a reception at a country club, where dinner was served and a local DJ entertained the guests.

The following day the two families flew to Texas, where there was a second reception that night in San Angelo. As the festivities finally ended and the newlyweds left on their honeymoon, Jack commented, "It would have been easier if the kids had just eloped. As I remember, Carole, our honeymoon was attending the county fair."

"Be serious, Jack. I know you want things to be better for our children than it was for us, just like I do," Carole said.

* * *

One month later, Liz was sitting in her room with the door open when Zuzu looked in. "Got a moment, Liz?" She asked.

"Sure. What can I do for you?"

"There was a big guy downstairs an hour ago, wearing a Stetson, talking to your dad. Do you know who he is?"

"Sure," Liz replied, "That's Rod Burkhart, the new foreman for the ranch where we lived when I was little."

"Do you know if he is married?"

"His wife died last year in a car wreck. He has a little two-year-old boy," Liz explained.

"Can you help me meet him?" Zuzu asked.

Liz thought for a moment and asked, "You lived in a commune a few years back, didn't you?"

"Well, yes. But what does that have to do with anything?"

"Both of you have experience with agriculture," Liz said. "But let's go talk to Dad." So, the two girls went downstairs, where Jack was reading a newspaper. "Dad," Liz asked, "how old is Rod?"

"According to papers he filled out when I hired him, he is thirty-eight," Jack replied as he dropped his paper. "And that's way too old for you, young lady."

Liz laughed. "I'm asking for Zuzu, Dad. She was curious, and I said I would find out."

"That's different," Jack said. "He noticed Zuzu in your mother's office the other day and asked me who she was."

Liz grabbed Zuzu's hand and said, "Let's go pay him a visit."

Zuzu was surprised and said, "We can't just barge in on him, Liz."

"Are you kidding? Of course I can. My dad owns the place. Let's go say hello," she said as the two girls left.

As the two girls hurriedly departed, Carole asked Jack, "Where are they leaving to in such a hurry?"

Jack rolled his eyes and said, "I guess Liz is playing matchmaker," as he again perused the paper.

Liz drove to Wall community, where the ranch was located. During the drive, Zuzu protested that they couldn't just drop in without a good reason, but Liz ignored her and reminded her that meeting Rod was her idea. Liz knocked on the door, and Rod opened it. "Well, Miss Curtis, what brings you out here?"

Liz smiled and calmly replied, "Zuzu is from New York and mentioned she has never seen a real ranch. So, I thought I'd see if you might show her around."

"Not a problem," Rod said. "Let me get Bronco, and I'll do that."

"Who's Bronco?" Zuzu questioned.

"That's his little boy," Liz replied.

In a few seconds, Rod returned, holding his son. "He's adorable!" Zuzu squealed.

"Let's hop in the pickup, and I'll show you around," Rod said. With Bronco sitting on Liz's lap, the four drove to the fence about forty yards behind the house. Rod asked a worker shoeing a horse to open the gate and then drove out into the pasture. About three hundred yards farther, there was a large water trough about thirty feet long. On one end was a pipe to refill it, and about forty cattle were around or near it. "There are five troughs like this around the four thousand acres the ranch encompasses, and they are refilled each morning," Rod explained.

"Who comes out to refill them?" Zuzu asked.

Rod laughed. "They're on a clock. We're in the twentieth century now. It would take too long to have them filled by hand."

As they continued to drive, Zuzu asked, "I thought cattle in Texas had extra-long horns?"

"The longhorn species produce very lean meat," Rod explained. "Traditionally, people complained longhorn cattle had fifty cents of hamburger on every hundred pounds of bone and horn. They're also very temperamental. The species we're raising are Angus. They provide a better quality of meat and are more docile."

About twenty minutes later, they were back at the residence. As they walked inside, Rod said, "It's almost dinner time," as he walked to the kitchen. "I can put some hamburgers on the grill if you two are as hungry as I am."

Zuzu winked at Liz and whispered, "Beat it, kid. I can handle things from here."

"Oh, Rod," Liz said, "Mom was expecting me back by now. If Zuzu stays, you will have to give her a ride back to her place."

"Not a problem," Rod said. "Tell your folks hello for me."

"Okay," Liz replied. "I'll see you tomorrow, Zuzu." Then, with a big smile, Liz winked at Zuzu and left.

Chapter Twenty-Seven

It was getting close to year's end, and Jack had spent the morning talking with his consultants. First, it was his CPA, and later with a financial adviser. There were no longer numerous trips to New York for Cayuga board meetings, but his life didn't seem to get any less complicated.

Now it was almost noon as he pulled into the driveway of his home. With the charities that Carole administered, she no longer cooked, and the cook she had hired insisted on serving meals promptly at scheduled times. Jack had ten minutes to get to the table. *It's ridiculous to be ordered around in my own home*, he thought.

"Guess who's getting married?" Carole said as he walked into the house.

Jack barely raised his hands in a half-hearted shrug showing a lack of interest, and replied, "Surprise me."

"It's Rod and Zuzu, and they want us to be witnesses," Carole replied with a big smile.

"What! That's impossible," Jack exclaimed. "He spent two years in Vietnam, and she used to be an anti-war protester. So, what in heaven's name could they have in common?"

"Apparently, love," Carole replied with her hands on her hips. "Be happy for them, Jack!"

"Okay, sweetheart, I'll throw them a party afterward if you insist."

Carole kissed him and said, "That's the spirit. We need more happiness in the world. Now let's eat lunch. Wilda has it ready for us."

They only used the large dining room for guests or special occasions. With Liz visiting friends, Jack and Carole sat at a small table on the far side of the kitchen where Wilda had everything ready. As they sat down, Jack said, "You ought to grab a plate and join us, Wilda."

"No sir, Mr. Curtis," Wilda replied. "That ain't proper. I'll eat after I take care of you folks."

As Jack reached for the potatoes, Carole hesitantly said, "Uh, Jack!"

"Oh yes," Jack replied and withdrew his hand. Since Wilda had been hired, she insisted the family return the thanks before eating. He folded his arms and said a short prayer, after which both Carole and Wilda added an amen.

"Remember, Mr. Curtis, it ain't right to eat food that ain't been blessed. If you don't thank the Good Lord for your bounty, he might stop providing it for you," Wilda admonished.

"Thank you, Wilda," Jack said in a reserved tone.

About an hour later, Jack drove out to the ranch. Rod was observing the delivery of some hay as he arrived. "Hello, Mr. Curtis," Rod said as Jack walked up. "What brings you out this way?"

"I understand congratulations are in order," Jack said, extending his hand. "I'm a little confused about one thing, though."

"What's that?"

"Well, Zuzu used to protest the war, and you served two tours in Vietnam. So, I'm a little surprised you two hit it off."

Rod sighed. "Mr. Curtis, deep down, I suspect you know as well as I that we had no business in that war."

"Now that it's over, I'm starting to feel like that," Jack agreed. "The way you men were kept on a short leash and fed into a political meat-grinder, with no real long-term plans or goals, was unforgivable," Jack agreed.

"Well," Mr. Curtis, "that's a good description of the war. "I love my country and was proud to serve in the army, but I'm disappointed we ever got involved in that conflict. If I had known then what I know now, I never would have."

With a quizzical look, Jack asked, "Why is that?"

Rod hesitated for a few seconds and replied, "After I was wounded in the battle of Hue, I spent time in the hospital, and when I got out, I was assigned my last few weeks to MACV. I learned some interesting facts there."

"Such as?" Jack questioned with interest.

"Well," Rob began. "When Kennedy put the first advisers in the country, they could only shoot in self-defense and we were very limited as to their activity. Our ally's name was Ngo Diem, and he was anti-Communist. One colonel told me that Kennedy only agreed because they shared similar views. However, when Diem started persecuting Buddhists, Kennedy got upset and thought of pulling out."

"I didn't know that," Jack said.

"It gets better," Rod added. "After Kennedy's death and Johnson took over, LBJ wanted to be a wartime president like his hero, FDR. So, he lied about our people being attacked in the Gulf of Tonkin and got Congress to authorize combat troops. You know the rest. Over fifty thousand of our people were killed afterward. I consider almost all of those Americans to have been personally murdered by President Johnson."

Jack considered what he had heard. "Are you telling me the battle in the Gulf of Tonkin never happened?"

"Mr. Curtis, a couple of Vietnamese sailed out and took a couple of shots at one of our ships. They didn't even scratch the paint on the boat. We then blew them out of the water. Of course, it was nothing, but Johnson pretended it was Pearl Harbor again. He just wanted to be a wartime president." Rod looked at Jack and said, "I'm proud of Zuzu for protesting. Maybe I wouldn't have had to go over there if more people had done it."

After reflecting on Rod's statement, Jack said, "I served in Europe from 1942 to '46. Things were a lot different there. Sadly, you guys didn't ever get a welcome home or a parade to thank you for your service."

They stood there for a few minutes discussing their military service and looking at the cattle in the distance, and when Rod added, "I wouldn't want this to go any further, since it makes people mad, but sometimes I suspect Johnson was behind the murder of President Kennedy."

"You might be right!" Jack exclaimed. "I've always despised the man; I could believe he engineered that assassination."

"You do? I thought I was the only one. So many people get mad when I think the president could be so corrupt."

"Rod, Johnson made Al Capone look like an innocent choir boy. Johnson would buy up worthless land in his wife's name and then have the government place an important building or complex next to it. Then his wife's worthless land became valuable commercial property. He's gotten rich that way."

"How do you know these things," Rod asked.

"I have friends in Austin that let me in on things like that. For example, if they tell me a government highway or project is planned, I will buy land nearby. I may be taking advantage of the information, but I'm not doing anything illegal. On the other hand, Johnson forced others to set things up so he could act afterward and screw other people over. He's used his power in the Senate to cheat others and make millions of dollars for himself."

"Wow!" Rod said. "I figured things were like that."

"It's even worse than that, Rod."

"How's that?"

"An FBI agent told me that in '61, Johnson's dealings with Bill Sol Estes were being investigated by an agricultural agent named Henry Marshal. Before Marshal could release his findings to a grand jury, he was found dead with a bolt action rifle that someone had used to shoot him five times. The local justice of the peace, one of Johnson's cronies, ruled the death a suicide."

Rob snorted a laugh. "That's unbelievable!"

"Unfortunately, it's true. Johnson paid off Estes to keep his mouth shut by providing for his family while he was in prison, and Estes' accountant was found dead in his car. Case closed."

"If you ever say anything, people will claim you're dealing in conspiracy theories," Rod noted. "It's best just to stay silent."

"That's probably for the best," Jack agreed, "I know you're not supposed to speak ill of the dead, and Johnson's been gone for four years, so I usually try to say something good. After all, he did get that civil rights bill passed."

"Yes, that's true," Rod concurred, "but before that, he spent thirty years in the Senate voting against civil rights bills. He even voted against the anti-lynching law. Any good he ever did for my people was canceled out by the bad." Rod added, "Maybe we should just forget the man altogether."

"Let's do that," Jack said. "By the way, Rod, I promised Carole I would throw you and Zuzu a party to celebrate your wedding. You two can invite as many friends as you like, and I'll pick up the tab. Where do you want to have the party?"

"I don't know. I guess your country club is out."

"Why?" Jack replied. "It's for members and guests, and you'd be my guest. So, you and Zuzu set the date, and I'll make it happen."

"Are you kidding? You'd do that for me?" Rod exclaimed.

"It's the least I can do for a fellow veteran and an excellent employee," Jack replied.

Rod grabbed Jack's hand and shook it as he said, "Mr. Curtis, thank you. I don't know what else to say."

Jack smiled and replied, "Say you'll continue to be a great manager of the ranch, a good husband to Zuzu, and in the future, just call me Jack."

"Yes sir, Jack. Thank you," Rod said as they hugged each other.

Chapter Twenty-Eight

Two weeks later, as the final arrangements were in place for what Jack called a party, Carole asked, "How did you manage to get the reception scheduled at the country club, Jack? I figured there was no way you could do that."

"It was simple, sweetheart. First, I didn't tell them for whom I scheduled it. Then, after they found out and wanted to cancel, I reminded them how much bad publicity they could get for canceling an event featuring a decorated veteran instead of the publicity they would receive for holding the event."

Carole gave a puzzled look and questioned, "Decorated veteran?"

"Yes, sweetheart," Jack sarcastically replied. "In two vacations in beautiful Southeast Asia, Rod received an ARCOM with a V device, a bronze star with an oak leaf cluster, a purple heart, a soldier's medal, and a CIB."

"What in the world is all that?" Carole asked.

"Sweetie, its medals and badges a soldier gets to put on his uniform after he gets shot at and survives. Rod received more than most." Then, with a smile, he added, "And I made it sound even more impressive than it was."

"I'll bet many members still won't like it, Jack."

With a shrug, her husband replied, "They'll get over it."

Carole got up from her seat, kissed him, and said, "I am so proud of you, and Liz thinks you're a hero."

Jack feigned a haughty look and replied, "The lord of the manor should always be revered as a hero. However, I'll excuse you from bowing and scraping in the future."

Carole laughed and said, "Ha! As if I would. I've been married to you long enough to know you're human, mister, and don't forget it."

With another phony look of anguish, Jack lamented, "Alas, the lord of the manor receives no respect from his subjects."

Carole continued to laugh at his antics. Then, before she returned to her desk, she kissed him again and said, "When you find those subjects, remind them that I'm the lady of the manor."

* * *

For the spring semester, Liz transferred to the University of Kansas. The departure technically left Jack and Carole as empty nesters. Ironically, however, they were not alone. In addition to a gardener, a housekeeper, and a cook, Carole hired two workers to assist in the charity work. So, they were never alone at home until evening.

Zuzu was no longer there each day. She was assisting her husband with the operation of the ranch. To stave off boredom, Jack had been elected to the city council. It only met twice a month, but he was involved with several projects around town.

Every three or four months, Jack and Carole would travel to Bedford Falls to visit friends and always visited the Baileys. On this latest trip, Jack was talking to Pete.

"For the first time in my life, I'm starting to get nervous, Jack," Pete explained. "The current trends in the economy are not promising."

"What's happening, Pete?"

"The current rate of inflation is causing some real problems. We are all right now, but some thrifts could go insolvent if the trends continue." Pete explained.

"Why is that?"

"The government sets the interest rates we pay on deposits," Pete explained. "If inflation continues to rise, people can get a better rate of return elsewhere, and folks may withdraw their money. Meanwhile, our income is primarily interest on long-term, fixed-rate mortgages. Those mortgages will lose considerable value if interest rates continue to rise."

Jack considered what Pete was saying and asked, "If the interest rates continue to rise, what is your strategy for the future?"

"First to pray that inflation cools off like it has in the past. If that doesn't happen, I'm hoping the government will deregulate us so we can have additional options."

"How can I help, Pete?"

"I'm aware that you know a few congressmen. See if you can get them to help us. Thrifts like ours have been a mainstay of the economy for almost a hundred years. The government needs to help us instead of causing pain," Pete suggested.

With a smile, Jack admitted, "I've always given campaign donations to both parties so I can approach each with equal access. I'll see what I can do. In the meantime, start writing up some proposed changes in the law that I can pass along to members of Congress."

"Thanks, Jack. I knew I could count on you."

Chapter Twenty-Nine

It was an exciting time as Liz was coming home at the end of the spring semester for her twenty-first birthday. It would occur the following day, and Jack and Carole had a huge birthday party planned. It was to be held at the country club. However, a few members were still angry about how Jack had managed to rent the main ballroom for the wedding of his ranch foreman and Zuzu. Those members had threatened to exclude him from renting the facility on future occasions, but again the possibility of bad publicity forced them to reconsider.

In his discussion with the club's general manager, Jack explained, "Well, Harman, now we can brag that our club doesn't discriminate."

The man replied with a few choice expletives and explained, "That's the point, Jack. We have this club so that we *can* discriminate."

"Well, the times, they are a-changin'," Jack said as he finalized the arrangements for Liz's party.

As it turned out, Liz had a big surprise for her parents. As she pulled up in front of the house, the gardener came in the side door and announced, "Mrs. Curtis, your daughter's here, and she has a passenger with her."

Carole quickly went to the front door as Liz and a young man came up the walk. She stepped outside to hug her daughter as

Liz held up her left hand to show off a large diamond ring. The slim, well-dressed young man with reddish-blond hair at her side said, "I'm Reg."

Carole instantly stopped and stood in shock as she considered the situation and observed the ring.

"Mother," Liz said, "meet Reginald Montgomery Bradwell." Then to the young man, she said, "This is my mother."

With a sheepish grin, Reggie said, "It's an honor to meet you, ma'am. I've been looking forward to this, and I apologize for Liz being so secretive. However. I've learned not to argue with her." He shook hands with Carole.

Still shocked, Carole said, "We can talk inside." She then assisted the two in bringing in their luggage as Liz said, "We can put them in my room."

"No," Carole said firmly. "Reginald will sleep in the guest room."

"Mother, seriously," Liz complained. "This is 1977, and we're consenting adults."

"Yes," Carole agreed. "And until you're married, you'll consent to sleep in separate rooms in my home."

Reggie laughed and said, "I agree, Mrs. Curtis, as my mother would say the same thing. Although, of course, Liz is a little more bohemian than I am, I assure you. I love your daughter dearly."

"I hope you know what you're in for, Reginald," Carole replied as she collected her thoughts. "She spent a lot of time around a former flower child. Now let me call her father."

Jack was concluding a real estate deal at the bank when Carole finally got in touch with him. After finishing his business, Jack hurried back home as she told him Liz had a big surprise for them. Numerous thoughts raced through his mind as he considered Carole's cryptic message.

Once home, the four spent time getting acquainted. Reg (as he preferred to be called) had just graduated with a law degree from Kansas and would be joining his father's law firm when he passed the bar exam. He also explained that his mother liked long, aristocratic names. "My two brothers' middle names are Archibald and Augustus, so that it could have been worse for me," he said. "I've decided Montgomery isn't bad, even though it sounds like a department store."

"Liz," her father said, "we are planning a big birthday party at the country club tomorrow night. So don't you two make other plans. I've spared no expense."

"Let's turn it into a wedding!" Liz shrieked with delight.

"Liz!" her mother gasped. "It takes a long time to plan a wedding. Your bridesmaids need to have matching dresses, you need to order a dress, and there are so many other items to take care of."

"Mother, please. We don't need to be bourgeois and provincial. I can buy a dress off the rack, and my friends can wear what they want."

"Liz, I insist on a certain amount of tradition," Carole demanded. "It must be a white, full-length dress, not a miniskirt. Tell your friends you want to be bridesmaids to go to that fashionable store downtown, buy a dress, and put it on our bill. Tell them what color you want so, hopefully, the whole affair won't look too haphazard."

As Carole continued to give orders, Reggie looked over at Jack and said with a laugh, "Your wife is just like my mother."

"Reg," Jack said, "some things you don't argue with your wife over. Carole has waited twenty-one years to plan Liz's wedding, and she will not be robbed of the chance. So don't you kids even think of eloping."

"I'll have to call my folks and have them hurry and catch a plane down here," Reggie said.

"Use the phone in my office upstairs," Jack replied. "Let's go up there." The two men then left Carole, who was hastily planning the wedding over Liz's objections.

"Fine, Mom, we'll do it your way," Liz acquiesced, "but I'll make a reservation for a good hotel room tomorrow night. I'm not spending my wedding night in my old bedroom."

"Good girl," her mother said. "Now we're thinking alike."

The entire confusion was abruptly ended when Wilda announced that dinner was ready. The four sat at the small table by the kitchen and continued to plan while they ate. Knowing Liz was old enough to get married over her parent's objections, Jack accepted the situation. He asked Reggie, "Where are you two going for your honeymoon."

"I don't know," he replied. "Where do you want to go for our honeymoon, Liz?"

Liz thought briefly and replied, "Let's go to Hawaii."

Jack looked at Reggie and commented, "The best thing about being a male is the only thing we have to plan is the entertainment we're going to provide for our lovely bride on the wedding night."

"Oh, Jack!" Carole started to protest. Unable to think of anything else to say, she paused as they heard Wilda laughing in the other room.

The entire wedding was able to come together far more painlessly than one would have expected. Fortunately, all the people needed already planned to attend Liz's birthday party. Reggie's parents were able to get an early flight to San Angelo, and at noon all six people were sitting around the formal table in the dining room.

Having not had much time to get acquainted, there was a brief conversation during the meal among the parents. Reggie's parents were Philip and Kathy Bradwell of Topeka. Philip had a large and successful law practice in Kansas. "I can see you have done very well for yourself and your family," Philip said to Jack.

"I have been very fortunate," Jack agreed. "I started with a little ranch I inherited from my father, and things went well from there. I have a lot to be thankful for."

"We understand, you operate a charity, Carole," Kathy acknowledged.

"Yes, there was a time when we didn't have much, so I want to help others," Carole replied. Reggie and Liz mostly remained silent as their parents awkwardly struggled for something to say.

That evening, Jack welcomed all who came. He introduced Reggie's parents and said a few words. He finished with, "Liz has always been a little impetuous and very unorthodox, and when she learned we had planned a birthday party, she instantly decided to change it to a wedding. Personally, I believe it was her way of getting around our rule requiring them to sleep in separate bedrooms while they were here." As people laughed, he added, "Liz doesn't want a reception line, so after the ceremony, we will enjoy dinner, and then a band will provide music so we can all dance and socialize. Thank you all for being here."

At that point, the minister took his place at the front of the room. Reggie and his father were to the preacher's left, and as an organist played the bridal march, Liz's friends came down the center aisle and lined up on his right. Then Jack led his daughter to her place by Reggie. Even though they had had no chance for a rehearsal, everything went well.

"You embarrassed me, Daddy," Liz said with a shy grin.

"Good, sweetie. Now we're even for your antics over the years." As he gave his daughter away, he had tears in his eyes as he kissed her on the cheek.

During the dance following the dinner, while Liz was talking to some of her friends and Carole was spending time with Reggie's parents, Jack pulled Reggie aside.

"Have you ever considered going into politics, Reg?" Jack asked.

"Yes, sir, I have. But I'm only twenty-five and barely finished law school. I need to get myself established in a law practice first to have a chance to be elected."

"Not necessarily," Jack told him. "A lot of times, a new face can attract a lot of attention. I know people who specialize in politics. I think you could do well with the right management and proper financing."

"Campaigns are expensive, and I don't think I could raise the money needed," Reg argued.

"I can provide the financing and introduce you to the right people." Then looking Reg straight in the eyes, he said, "Think about it, and we can talk later. Next year is an off-year election. So at least consider it."

As Reg realized Jack was serious, he replied, "I will, sir. Thank you."

At ten P.M., Jack made an announcement. "As this wedding was a spur of the moment and rather haphazard, we will invite you to a special banquet in two weeks at the Heritage House Restaurant for a more formal wedding dinner. This event was supposed to be a birthday party, but my nonconformist and unconventional daughter turned it into a wedding at the last moment."

Liz tossed her bouquet at eleven, and the couple left to their motel. Two of Liz's friends collected the birthday gifts, and then Reggie's parents went to Jack and Carole's home, where they could relax after a busy day.

The two couples sat at the small table by the kitchen the following morning and enjoyed a leisurely breakfast. As Wilda ensured everyone's coffee cup remained full, Phillip asked Jack, "What do you attribute your success to, Jack? You've said you were very fortunate, but I think it has been more than that."

"I have always sought advice from the best sources I could find." Jack began. "Our society is changing. Where people used to go into town to shop, now so many live in the suburbs that malls strategically placed gain much of the business that otherwise might have gone downtown." After another sip of coffee, Jack continued. "You look at a map and figure where the next sub-divisions will be built, and you buy the land in that area."

"Does it always work out?" Phillip asked.

"Sometimes not so well," Jack admitted. "You figure a road is going in, and you buy land in that area, and some politician reroutes the road for his own purposes."

"Jack also does well with stocks," Carole said proudly.

"That's more of a crap shoot," Jack said. You read the trade papers and look for a promising small company getting ready to expand or go public. If you pick the right one and it is successful, you can make a killing." Jack changed the subject and asked Phillip, "How about you? You seem to have done quite well also."

"I have also had some good fortune. Several clients have sought my assistance, and my expertise in the law has paid dividends," Phillip explained.

"If I could go back and do it all over, I think I might have gone into the oil business," Jack said retrospectively. "Men like

J. Paul Getty and H. L. Hunt are multi-billionaires. But, having done it my way, I'm only worth a fraction of that." He smiled, and added with a chuckle, "If I were a billionaire, Carole would have a lot more money to give away."

"The oil fields are dangerous, Jack," Carole noted. "I'm glad you did things the way you did."

"Ranching is dangerous, too, Carole, and a lot less profitable," Jack said with a sigh.

Chapter Thirty

Jack hired a political consulting firm to advise him on the congressional race where Reg and Liz were living. The congressman in their district was popular and well financed. However, in the district whose boundary was just eight miles to their west, it was a different story. The man who held that seat was older and was seen by many as inattentive to constituents' needs. The report showed that if he faced serious opposition, he might retire. Jack made his move.

Meeting with Reg, during a visit to Topeka, Jack explained the situation. "If you move to the upscale subdivision just over eight miles to the west, your commute to work will increase only a half hour, and you will be a viable candidate in that district. You wait until the last day to file and then have a meeting with the press, and here is the speech you need to give," Jack explained. He then emphasized the following: "You must appear to be speaking from the heart rather than giving a speech. It will do more harm than good if you look like you're reading or reciting a memorized speech. Do you understand?"

"Yes, sir," Reg replied. "I can do it."

After Reg filed for office, the incumbent congressman retired. Four others were vying for the seat, but only one was in the opposite party. Reg was instructed not to criticize his fellow party members, and when he narrowly won the primary he got their endorsement and cruised to victory with help from his advisers.

On election night, Jack and Carole were in Topeka to help his daughter and son-in-law celebrate. "Oh, Daddy! Thank you so much!" Liz gushed. "I am so excited! We couldn't have done it without you."

"You are welcome, young lady," Jack said. "Now, you must ensure you don't do anything controversial to hurt your husband's career."

"Daddy," she said in an irritated manner, "I am who I am. I do things my way and resent being told what to do. I love Reggie and he knows I'll be an asset, not a liability."

Jack quickly apologized. "I'm sorry, Liz, I didn't mean that the way it came out. I know you're intelligent and you like to help people. Reggie is very lucky to have my little girl beside him."

Liz said with a disdainful look, "I'm not little anymore, Daddy. I'm almost two years older than Mom was when you married her."

"Yes, you're a beautiful person, and I'm proud of you," Jack said. "Your mother has suggested the possibility of setting up a branch of her charity here in Kansas. You could run that, and assist your husband, until you two get busy and provide us with some grandchildren."

"Oh, Daddy," Liz giggled, "you're as bad as mother."

After Reg took office in January, Jack and Carole were there as he took his seat in Congress. While Carole talked to Liz, Jack waited for his chance to speak to Reg.

"Reg," he said when they were alone, "there are a lot of people that need your help. The savings and loan associations around the country are hurting, not only in Texas and Kansas but elsewhere else, as well. They need legislation to help them." Reaching into his pocket, he said, "Here is the phone number for Pete Bailey, who runs a large savings and loan in Bedford Falls in New York State. He can tell you better than I what is needed. Please contact him. He is expecting your call, and if you team up with his congressman in New York, I think you two can do a lot to solve the problem."

"Thanks, Jack. I'll see what I can do," Reg said.

A little while later, Jack called Pete. "Pete, I gave my son-in-law your number. If you explain what is needed, hopefully, he can help you get the savings and loan business back on track."

"Thanks, Jack," Pete replied. "I've been talking with our congressman here, and he is looking for others to help sponsor the legislation. So, I think we are on our way. I appreciate your help."

"You are welcome, Pete. I have also been bending the ears of our Texas representative members of Congress, so you should have plenty of sponsors for that legislation. Best of luck."

"Thanks again, Jack. I am indebted to you."

Sadly, despite Jack's good intentions for the savings and loan industry, the future would not be bright. Sometimes, despite hard work and sound designs, desires, and goals, tragically, things do not work out.

Chapter Thirty-One

It was 1980 before Congress passed the legislation Pete Bailey was seeking. Like all congressional legislation, it had a lengthy title. The bill had the verbose name of The Depository Institutions Deregulation and Monetary Control Act of 1980.

Unfortunately, in the intervening years since 1977, a new problem had been arising. This issue ultimately became known as the zombie thrifts. With the increasing interest rates and rising inflation, these thrifts began sustaining considerable losses. They then began investing in riskier investments, as allowed by the deregulation. When it became clear that these institutions were insolvent, regulators became fearful that shutting down these financial loan associations would cause a national panic of bank runs. The discovery that compounded this hesitance was the knowledge that losses could amount to twenty-five billion dollars, while the insurance fund available had only five billion dollars available. Therefore, the regulators decided to see if the problem institutions could *grow* out of their problems.

These zombie thrifts then offered higher deposit rates to gain the capital to grow out of the difficulty. They then engaged in a "go for broke" strategy of investing in riskier and riskier projects with the new funds. Unfortunately, that policy was disastrous.

Sadly, the most significant number of zombie thrifts was occurring in Texas. Savings and loan managers there were more reckless and accepting of risk and saw their businesses fail at an alarming rate. Now Pete called Jack, and there was concern in his voice.

"Jack, what in the world is going on in Texas? If that continues, it could take the entire industry down."

"I'm sorry, Pete. I wish I had made some friends with the savings and loan people here in my home state. From what I have discovered, there are a bunch of riverboat gamblers down here who think they are invincible. They have friends who are more powerful than I am. Those friends have convinced them that the government will bail them out and there is nothing to fear."

"There is a lot to fear, Jack. Unfortunately, the problem in Texas is spreading to the rest of the country, and we are in trouble."

"You told me how your father survived the Depression by keeping his head and paying attention to detail. You can weather this, Pete. The economy always improves."

"Look, Jack, I'm starting to hear about derivatives. What do you think about them?"

"Pete, I would not touch them with a ten-foot pole. They are a zero-sum investment, meaning you have a fifty percent chance of losing. No self-respecting gambler would touch them, so you shouldn't risk your depositor's money on them."

"Okay, thanks. I appreciate the information. But see if you can get congressmen on your end to come up with some relief to the problem, because we need all the help we can get."

As he hung up the phone, Carole asked, "Are things as bad as what I heard on your end sounds?"

"I hate to say so, Carole, but yes, they are. This goody-two-shoes president has now turned our national economy into the Titanic. Fortunately, we'll be rid of him come election time."

"Do you think the next president will be any better, Jack?"

"Carole, sweetheart, it is impossible for the next president to do worse. So things can only get better," Jack reassured.

At least in the short term, Jack was wrong, as politicians got involved. A son of the country's new vice president was on a Colorado thrift board and was sued for ethical problems and conflicts of interest. Also, a Texas congressman resigned in disgrace after intervening in the crises to help friends who used the system for personal gain, and several senators were bribed to help friends whose thrifts were insolvent. Soon half of the country's thrifts had gone out of business.

* * *

One morning, a well-dressed gentleman entered the Central New York Savings and Loan's main office. He had been recommended to Pete by other businessmen in the New York area. As he entered Pete's office, he introduced himself.

"Mr. Bailey, I'm Ryan Campbell, and it is a pleasure to meet you. I spoke to Congressman Kowalski yesterday, and he sends his best."

"Yes," Pete replied. "The congressman speaks highly of you. Please have a seat and let me know what I can do for you."

"Mr. Bailey, it's what I can do for you. I have formed a company that mines rhodium."

"Rhodium?" Pete responded. "I've never heard of it. What is it and what is it used for?"

The man smiled as he relaxed in the chair before Pete's desk and explained, "It is the most expensive and rarest of precious metals. It is currently more than twice as expensive as gold and destined to increase exponentially."

Pete sat up and leaned forward. Eager to hear more, as Mr. Campbell continued. "Currently, with our government insisting that cars not pollute the air, it is used in catalytic converters to reduce pollutants. However, as technology improves, rhodium could become far more useful in other items. However, increasing the number of vehicles on the road will guarantee its necessity and increased value."

Pete asked, "I would have to do a lot of research before investing in something as speculative as mining."

"Excellent point, sir," the man said. "To minimize risk, we also have a hedge fund with over a half billion dollars set up."

"I'm also not very familiar with hedge funds," Pete replied.

"A hedge fund is a pooled investment fund that trades in relatively liquid assets," Campbell explained. "We extensively use more complex trading, portfolio-construction, and risk-management techniques to improve performance. We do extremely well with short-selling, leverage, and derivatives." Campbell then emphasized the following, "Due to the complexities of the business, financial regulators restrict hedge fund marketing to institutional investors, high net worth individuals, and accredited investors, like me." He smiled and ended his spiel with, "Obviously, hedge fund investment is not available to everyone. However, a business like yours, which has pooled funds from the members, qualifies and allows smaller investors to enjoy the same benefits of investing that our society's billionaires enjoy."

Pete strained in his mind to digest the information he had just heard. It sounded like a lot of gobbledygook, but he quickly asked a question. "How is the rhodium mine connected to the hedge fund investing?"

"Excellent question, sir," Campbell replied. "Many investors want their vested interests to be based on an actual commodity, and with the anticipated increased value of rhodium, there is none better. Between the land holdings we have and with the valuable mineral we are mining, any fears can be set aside for the guarantee of high returns."

"I would have to investigate and check with other individuals investing with your company," Pete stated.

"Sir, I would insist upon it. Of course, one must always do their due diligence. After all, if a deal is good today, it will still be excellent in the future. The only difference is that you'll miss out on some high returns in the meantime. I will leave you with a list of clients you can check to verify what I'm saying."

"Thank you," Pete said as they shook hands. After Campbell left, he made some calls and learned others were receiving a fifteen percent return on their money. He also called a geology professor at a local college and asked about a mineral called rhodium.

The professor verified what Pete had been told. "Some experts think the price of rhodium could more than double in the next five years," he said.

Chapter Thirty-Two

As Jack's net worth grew, Carole encouraged him to direct more assets toward charitable endeavors. By 1986, the recession appeared to be over, as inflation finally dropped to less than two percent. It was down some eleven points from ten years earlier. So, in this environment, the families led by Jack and Pete prospered.

Legislation pushed by Reggie and his fellow members of Congress worked well for Pete. The deregulation of the savings and loan industry allowed thrifts to offer a more comprehensive array of savings products and significantly expanded their lending authority. In short, the legislation permitted thrifts like the one managed by Pete Bailey to grow out of their problems. In addition, the government explicitly sought to influence thrift profits instead of promoting housing and home ownership. The future looked bright as other changes authorized more lenient accounting rules and eliminated many legal restrictions previously in place. As a result, the Central New York Savings and Loan was having its best year despite national trends.

Meanwhile, in San Angelo, Jack's investments in land and oil were paying off handsomely. Carole argued that he should put more money into helping others. "Really, Jack," she argued, "many people are hurting and need help. We need to do more to assist others."

"Carole," he replied, "I buy small companies and expand them. That provides jobs for others so they can improve themselves. That is how I help my fellow human beings."

"But we need to do more," Carole demanded.

"Honey," he explained. "I don't want other people to become like my friend Vick."

"Who's he?"

"He was a neighbor when we were kids. He thought it was too much trouble to walk to school, so most of the time, he didn't go. Then when he dropped out after the tenth grade, his grandmother thought work was too hard for her *little boy*. So, since she was on relief and was provided for by others, he wound up the same way. Taxes paid by others provided for him until he drank himself to death, and good riddance."

"Apparently, he needed help, Jack!"

"He *chose* not to get educated and learned not to work, so I had no sympathy for him. Fortunately, the county took his grandmother's property in payment for the welfare they received and paid to cremate him. I'm guessing they threw his ashes into the landfill."

"That's terrible, Jack!"

"It's what he deserved, Carole. The Bible says if you will not work, you shall not eat. I believe in that. If someone refuses to work to improve themselves, they should get no help from others."

"We should always do what we can for others, regardless of the circumstances," his wife urged.

"Honey," he said in agitation, "if all the Vicks of the world were lined up and I gave them money until I was flat broke, they would still be poor in a week, and we would not have the resources to help them." Then, with emphasis, he added, "In that event, we would be as poor as they were, and they would still demand that we help them."

"Are you afraid of being poor again, Jack?" she said as she drew close to him.

He smiled at his wife. "Yes, sweetheart, I suppose I am. There were so many times I had to do without when I was a kid. Then we were close to losing the ranch after we helped Dewey and April. That changed after Uncle Henry died, and I never want to be in that position again."

Carole smiled and said, "I grew up poor, too, and I feel we should help others and be a little less judgmental."

Tomorrow would be Thanksgiving, and the extended Bailey family had come to Texas for the holiday. Mary and Carole were admiring David and Emma's three children. "How do you like being a great-grandmother, Mary?" Carole asked.

"It's similar to being a grandmother, except you know you're getting older," Mary replied. "I wish George was alive to see those born after his passing. He would be so proud."

"Yes, he would be," Carole agreed.

At the same time, Jack and Pete watched a football game with Reggie upstairs. David entered the room and asked Pete, "I just heard on the radio that a big thrift in California has gone under from risky real estate investments. That won't affect you, will it?"

"It shouldn't. We aren't in the same investments they were." Then, noticing a look of puzzlement on the others' faces, he explained, "The government wants everyone to be a homeowner, so they are trying to get thrifts to accept loans from customers who are not qualified to borrow the money. So far, we have resisted the pressure to do that."

"That's crazy!" Jack exclaimed. "Why on earth would they do that?"

Pete smiled. "We're dealing with the government here," he said. "They're bundling many mortgages and selling them as a fund backed by the government. Hopefully, as the economy improves, most people will become solvent enough for these funds to pay off. But, unfortunately, the rate of return is high enough many managers are willing to overlook the risk. I am not one of them."

"What investments are your business's funds in?" David asked.

"I invested heavily in a hedge fund operated by Ryan Campbell called the Pan-American Capital Growth Fund. They own rhodium mines in Montana and Canada. For us, the future looks great."

"What in the world is rhodium?" Reggie asked. "I've never heard of it."

"It is the rarest and most valuable mineral on earth," Pete explained. "It's far more valuable than gold. So, I figured I can't go wrong with a commodity like that backing my investments up."

Chapter Thirty-Three

It was Monday. December 26, 1990. Wilda had the day off and Jack and Carole had slept in. Now Jack was looking at his bowl grid picks he had for his entry in the contest the local paper sponsored each year. In the two games played so far, he had picked losers. *It's a good thing I didn't bet any money on this*, Jack thought as he read about yesterday's game. He tossed the paper aside and picked up a trade bulletin he had received just three days earlier.

An article on page three caught his eye. It detailed how a large mining consortium in the United Kingdom had purchased mining interests from a hedge fund for a quarter of a billion dollars.

He read with interest that Pan-American Capital Growth Fund had sold their interests, mining for a mineral called rhodium, and he recalled that was the name of the fund in which Pete had his thrift's investments. As Jack read, first he marveled how Pete's savings and loan must be doing well, as their investment was receiving such a large sum. Then it occurred to him that Pete had been impressed that the hedge fund was backed up by a precious metal, and wondered how the sale of the mining interests affected the value of that investment. He decided to give Pete a call.

As he dialed the number, he mused how making such a call had become much easier in the past thirty-one years. As a thrift employee answered the call, he asked for Pete, who was quickly on the phone.

"Hello, Jack," he said. "Did you folks in Texas have a Merry Christmas?"

"Yes, we did. The kids are both with their in-laws, so it was quiet. They will be coming to visit in a couple of days. Was Santa good to you and Pam?"

"We have no complaints," Pete said. "But what can I do for you today?"

Jack got right to the point, "I was reading in *Western Investing Today* that your hedge fund just sold their mining businesses," Jack explained. "I was wondering if you knew that."

"No, I didn't. I'll call Ryan Campbell and check things out. Thanks for the heads-up."

"You're welcome, Pete. How's everything else going?"

Pete assured him all was going well, and after a little small talk the call ended. Pete then called Campbell's office and learned the man was out of town on business. The office assistant told Pete that the sale put a quarter of a billion dollars in the fund and they could now diversify much more and be more profitable. As he hung up the phone, Pete got a bad feeling in his gut. The assistant's statement contradicted everything Campbell had previously discussed with him.

He quickly called a friend who knew individuals at the Resolution Trust Corporation overseeing insolvent thrifts.

"Tom," he said as he got the man on the phone, "have you heard anything about Pan-American Capital Growth Fund? I'm having trouble getting their top man on the phone."

"What's your interest in Pan-American, Pete?"

"My thrift has a lot of money invested with them, and I just heard they sold their mining interests. I am getting the feeling something is wrong. If you know anything, please tell me," Pete pleaded.

In a low voice, the friend hesitated and said, "I'm not at liberty to say anything, so you did not hear this from me, but the SEC is looking at them. There have been complaints that some investors have had trouble getting their money."

"Oh, my gosh," Pete moaned.

"As I said before, Pete, I never told you anything. You did not hear this from me. I just hope they find nothing wrong in their investigation."

After hanging up, Pete made other calls but could not locate Campbell, as Pan-American personnel kept giving him the runaround. Then three days later, it was breaking news on all media networks that the FBI had frozen Pan-American's assets, and Ryan Campbell had been arrested before he could board a flight to Brazil. His large suitcase contained several million dollars in negotiable bonds.

Then the news got worse. The federal investigators disclosed that the Pan-American Capital fund was a Ponzi scheme. Ryan Campbell had used a minority interest in a rhodium mine to lure investors in, and as more people joined the hedge fund, he used some funds from new investors to pay older investors. Then when a major investor wanted his money, Campbell sold his interest in the mine to obtain the funds to meet the obligation.

The sale took time, and because of the delay in meeting the debt, others began to ask questions, and federal regulators became involved. The smooth-talking Campbell kept them at bay for a while, but as investigators discovered more irregularities, he attempted to flee the country.

Ryan Campbell was now in jail and denied bond as a flight risk. A securities dealer who had energetically hawked the investment committed suicide, and others were in seclusion as the government regulators inventoried Campbell's assets. As they did so, they found millions of dollars were missing, and fear spread among the fund's investors that they had lost their life savings.

Pete started receiving calls from the press. They asked questions about his Pan-American Capital investments. He calmly tried to downplay the situation. "Yes, the Central New York Savings and Loan had some funds with Pan-American, but that was only a part of our investments." He assured everyone there was nothing to worry about. But, in his heart, he knew better.

Now Pete didn't know where to turn. His wife Pamela was still mourning the loss of their youngest grandchild, Gerald. Just six weeks before, the boy had been hit by a car while riding his bicycle. He passed away eight days later. While the sadness of the situation burdened Pete, the effect was worse on Pamela. The smiling, perpetually cheerful boy had been her pride and joy. Now, she was depressed and had trouble talking without breaking out in tears.

Unable to ask anyone for advice, he felt alone. The employees were worried about losing their jobs as well as their money, and all he could do was smile and tell them that everything would be all right. Unfortunately, his public smile betrayed his internal fear that he would be reviled by many as a failure and the man who had lost their money. The feeling of doom was all-encompassing. He began to feel he had no way out. Then, federal investigators had announced that shareholders could receive pennies on the dollar of their invested money. The savings and loan business the

Bailey family had run for about a hundred years might soon be declared insolvent.

Now Pete could take no more. He quickly left the office and went home, where he could no longer be stoic. The pressure was now too much. He entered the house crying. Pam had never seen her husband cry before. Even at the funeral of their grandson, he had put his arm around her and let her mourn for them both. He had always been the brave one.

"Pete, what's wrong?" she asked, as he continued to cry.

He put his hands up to his head as if he thought his brain might explode. With a look of wide-eyed terror he explained, "All the investments in Pan-American Capital are worthless. The savings and loan will be declared insolvent. Everyone will hate me for losing their money." He collapsed on the couch as he continued to cry.

Suddenly, Pam's thoughts of grief for her grandson disappeared as she approached her husband. "Sweetheart," his wife asked, "I'm sure you didn't do anything illegal."

"No, I didn't," he wailed as he sat up to explain. "But I trusted people who did. I will be blamed for this disaster. People put their faith in me, and I have let them down. Almost a billion dollars is gone, and it's my fault."

"I'm sure it can't be that bad, Pete," she protested as she put her arms around him. She hugged him and tried to console him as she repeated, "It can't be that bad."

"It is, Pam. It is," he sobbed. "The worst part is, I have failed my father. He saved the business from Potter in the Depression, and now I've lost it. I'm a failure and a total loser." He stood up and began to pace. The entire time, he cried about letting everyone in Bedford Falls down.

Pamela tried to calm him down, but he became even more irrational. "The broker that encouraged everyone to buy the fund has killed himself. He couldn't bear the news. So now everyone who bought on his advice will wish they were dead since he's not around to blame. If I weren't around, you and the kids would not have to bear the shame of this mess."

"Peter!" she yelled. "You need to relax. We can get through this."

As Pete realized he was upsetting his wife, he became determined to regain his more sober and impassive countenance. He sat down and feigned a calm presence. He forced a smile while his brain and emotions wanted to scream about the unfairness of the situation. His change of demeanor also briefly put Pam at ease.

Then, with the turmoil taking place in his brain, Pete got up and began to pace back and forth, trying to think. Then he saw Pamela's pills over by the kitchen sink. A calm feeling came over him as he walked over to them and made his decision. After he drank a glass of water, he smiled and said, "You're right, darling. Things will be alright. I need to get some legal advice." He kissed her and quickly left.

Pamela's brief relief at his suddenly more peaceful presence ended when she noticed that the bottle of pills she had been prescribed for insomnia and depression was missing. "Peter!" she screamed and ran for the door. But, unfortunately, he had already driven away.

Chapter Thirty-Four

A surge of absolute panic permeated Pam's body as she considered her husband's final words before he left the house. She immediately called Mary, practically hysterical as she attempted to tell Mary her concern as she shrieked, "I'm worried about Pete," into the phone.

"Calm down, Pam. Calm down," Mary said. "Relax and tell me what the problem is," she slowly said.

"Pete came home crying, saying he had lost a lot of money and the savings and loan would be out of business. I tried to get him to relax, but he said he's let his father down, and everyone will hate him."

"I'm sure it can't be that bad, Pam," Mary reassured.

"That's what I told him, and he told me people are killing themselves. I hugged him, and he got calm and said he needed legal help. But after he left, I noticed he had taken the bottle of pills I had by the sink." She continuing crying and said, "He seemed so desperate. I think he is going to do something terrible." As she continued screaming, she said, "I'm scared, and I don't know what to do."

"Let's start calling people and see if anyone has seen him," Mary counseled. "Once we know where he is, we can assure him things will improve. Somebody has to have seen him, so let's check with everybody he knows. Once we know where he is, we can reason with him."

After Mary hung up the phone, she prayed that nothing serious or tragic would happen to her son. Then, as she considered whom to call first, she thought of their friends in Texas. So she dialed the number for Carole.

As she answered the phone and listened to Mary, Carole tried to be supportive. "I'm sure Pete will be alright, Mary. He's far too intelligent to do anything rash."

Jack set down the paper he was reading and asked, "What's going on, sweetheart?" Carole handed the phone to Jack, who listened as Mary explained her concerns.

"Mary, I think this has to do with that crook who tried to skip the country a few days ago, and Pete had money invested with him," Jack explained. "Find Pete, and we will be there in a few hours to help in any way we can."

"Jack," Mary exclaimed. "It's New Year's Eve! I don't want to put you folks out."

"Mary," Jack explained, "I bought a plane three years ago, and I have a pilot who complains I don't give him enough flight time. So we will be there in a few hours."

Carole smiled. "You're passing up the party at the country club, honey?"

"Yes," he replied. "We have friends who need us. So, grab a suitcase and our toothbrushes, and I will call Steve."

Jack called his pilot, apologized for the late notice, and, after explaining the situation, invited Steve to have his family join them for the flight to celebrate in New York. "Jack," the man said, "my kids or old enough to want to party with their friends, but my wife will be happy to join us. I'll go get the plane ready."

Two hours later, Jack and Carole were in Jack's Cessna Citation at the San Angelo airport. While not a pilot, Jack sat up front with Steve Powell while the latter went through his preflight check. Carole and Steve's wife Margaret conversed in the front two seats of the ten-seat plane. A short time later, they were on their way.

* * *

Meanwhile, in Bedford Falls, Pete bought a bottle of whiskey at a liquor store. He wondered if he should buy a pint or a fifth, finally deciding on the former. Pete thought, *The Bailey Building and Loan—now the Central New York Savings and Loan—is insolvent after a hundred years*. He kept repeating the thought in his mind that he had failed. He had failed his family, his city, and his employees. He was a loser. He had no reason to continue to live.

As he returned to his car, his first thought was where to go for his final hours. After driving around, he remembered the family cabin at the lake. The area was usually snowed in this time of the year, but if he could get there, he knew he would be alone. *That would be fitting*, he thought. *If you are a loser, you should die alone.*

To his surprise, the road had been cleared recently. The fresh snow was not deep enough to prevent the car from reaching the cabin. However, before the last snow, a snowplow had left a large pile blocking the driveway, so he parked next to it and walked the final steps to the building. He walked around back, where a key was hidden, and he entered the cabin. The thermostat was set at forty degrees to prevent the pipes from freezing, so he turned it to a comfortable temperature. *Might as well have some comfort in my final hours, he thought.*

He opened the bottle of bourbon and took a swig. He sat for a moment and had a total calm come over him as he took another drink. *Time to get it over with*, he thought as he opened the bottle of pills. Then he was so surprised by the sudden appearance of another person in the room that he dropped the bottle of pills, which spilled on the floor. The vision was his father, George Bailey, except he looked about thirty years old. He was not the older man Pete remembered,

The apparition raised his hand and said, "Stop, son! It's not your time to leave. You have a family that needs you. You can do much by leading and setting a proper example for them."

Pete rubbed his eyes. He knew he had not drunk enough alcohol to be hallucinating. So he exclaimed, "Dad?"

"Yes, it's me, Pete."

"You died about twenty years ago," Pete said. "How can you be here?"

George smiled and said, "Yes, I left mortality eighteen years ago, but I still exist and am looking forward to seeing my family and friends again. However, this is not the time for you to join me."

"Dad!" Pete cried. "The thrift you and grandpa built is broke. I have lost all the money. There is nothing for me to live for. I am a disgrace to our family and friends."

"Nonsense," George said in a loud voice. "Money is worthless after this life. It means nothing in the eternities. Those who use it as a substitute for true happiness on earth suffer forever. People like Henry Potter will spend all time begging for forgiveness from those they mistreated. All you did was make an honest mistake and be beguiled by someone who will suffer an eternity of shame. You can hold your head up high and do whatever you can to rectify that situation here on earth."

"Dad, I don't have the money to replace what has been lost. How can I do that?"

In a soft, loving voice, his father smiled and said, "Son, while you are alive, you have the resources to do as much as possible. After you pass from this life, that chance is gone, and you can do nothing."

"But Dad," Pete asked, "what good can I do? If many people are angry and bitter after my mistake, why would my family care about the example I set?"

"Because they love you, Pete. They know you are a human being, and that's not a crime." The apparition waved his hand, and a scene unfolded before them. It was the bedroom of Pete's granddaughter, 16-year-old Julie. She was crying.

"Four months after your death," George explained, "a boy from the senior class she thinks she's in love with will dump her and call her names. Her heart is broken." Pete watched the vision.

"I can't believe he called me those names," the girl sobbed. "He even said I was ugly." She went to her closet and retrieved a long sash from a robe. "Grandpa showed me how to end the pain. I know what to do. That boy will regret dumping me. I'll show him." Standing on a chair, she quickly tied one end around her neck and the other to the overhead light fixture. Then she stepped off the chair.

"No, Julie, no!" Pete screamed, as the vision faded.

"If you were there," George calmly said, "you would put your arm around her and explain that before a young girl meets her handsome prince, she usually has to kiss a good many toads. Then she would forget that boy for good in a few weeks."

"If I'm not there, Dad, how much worse can it get?"

Then another vision materialized. The scene is Pete's funeral, and a well-dressed man approaches his widow Pam. The two talk briefly and leave together.

"That's Ashley Wilkinson," Pete exclaims. "He's about to be indicted for real estate fraud. So why would Pam have anything to do with him?"

George answered, "The answer is simple, Pete. She was already terribly depressed, and with your death, she is now completely vulnerable. He will convince her to sell the beautiful home you two shared, cash in your life insurance, and leave town. He will take the money and desert her in Buffalo, where she will spend several days in a homeless shelter until your children find her."

The scene played out until Pete begged, "I can't watch anymore. Please stop it."

"There's more," George said. "The two grandsons you coached in baseball last year will die in a New York City crack house two years from now because they no longer have the influence of your presence."

"I don't want to see that," he screamed. Then, looking at George, he said, "What do I have to do now, Dad?"

The spirit replied with a friendly, loving voice, "You know the answer to that, Pete. Continue to be yourself. Acting with honesty and integrity has always been how you do things, and I must add that you're even a better businessman than I was. Your grandpa and I have always been proud of you."

"Thanks, Dad."

"Now go," George said, "and have a long and happy life with Pamela. Farewell, until I see you again."

Pete wanted to talk more, but before he could speak, the vision faded. Then feeling completely exhausted, fell down on the couch and was quickly asleep.

* * *

Jack's plane landed at the Bedford Falls airport at 3:34 P.M. He quickly rented a car and went to the hotel, where he reserved two rooms. He then asked for the general manager, who promptly responded.

"Yes, Mr. Curtis, how may I serve you?" the man asked.

"I would like to introduce my good friends Steve and Margaret Powell. I've explained that your hotel throws the best New Year's Eve party in the State of New York. Unfortunately, I have to leave to take care of some family business, but anything they need should be put on my bill, and I will leave them in your care."

"Yes," the manager said. "I will see that a table is reserved for the four of you." He then turned to the Powells and said, "If you folks need anything special, just let me know."

Jack then said to Carole, "I'll be back as soon as possible."

Carole grabbed her husband's arm and said, "I'm coming with you, Jack. As desperate as Mary sounded on the phone, I'm sure I can help."

"I don't have time to argue, sweetheart, so let's go," He replied.

Steve, who had been briefed on the flight of the situation, said, "Good luck, Jack. We'll be praying everything works out fine."

"Yes, and thanks for everything, Jack," Margaret said.

It was now snowing, but Jack drove as quickly as he dared to Mary Bailey's house. She was talking with Pam, who was hysterical as he and Carole arrived. Mary explained what she had learned, as Carole hugged Pam and assured her everything would work out.

Mary said, "I have been calling everyone I know, and a few people have seen him. One said they had seen him at the midtown liquor store earlier, and Pete seemed in a hurry. And then Fred Sorenson said he saw him driving toward the lake road. That area is usually closed this time of the year, but he said they are trying to keep it open this year. So I think Pete might be going to the summer cabin." She added, "I don't drive in the snow, and Pam isn't in any condition to drive, so we had to wait for you, since the police all are busy with accidents and such."

"Let's get going," Jack said. "Mary, you sit up front and give me directions, and Carole can assure Pam everything will be fine in the back seat. With that, the four of them ventured out into the weather.

At a little past five, Jack turned onto the road by the lake. The snow started falling heavier, but he put the car in low gear and proceeded. A short time later, they saw Pete's car. After parking behind it, Jack and Carole helped Mary over the pile of snow blocking the driveway, and the four of them went to the door, which Mary quickly unlocked.

Pam was the first to hurry inside, and she screamed, "Oh no! We're too late," as she ran to her seemingly comatose husband and knelt at his side. The three others followed her. "Why, Pete? Why did you do it?" she sobbed.

"Why did I do what?" Pete said as he woke up and looked around.

The four others stood there in shock as Pam yelled, "You're alive? But you took those pills."

"I'm sorry, Pam. I accidentally spilled them on the floor . Here, I'll pick them up," he said.

"No you don't. But, thank God, you're alive!" She hugged him.

"I hate to change the subject, but by now, we're probably snowed in here," Jack said. "We probably ought to make ourselves comfortable," as he started picking up the pills while Mary joined Pam in hugging Pete.

Pete began to tell the unbelievable story about his experience when, after six o'clock, there was a honking noise outside. Jack ran to the door where a snowplow operator was standing next to his vehicle cursing a few expletives. "These cars are in my way," he yelled in colorful language. "I need to hurry and get home. It's New Year's Eve."

Jack pulled a hundred-dollar bill out of his wallet and said to the man. "If you can widen this part of the road where we can get turned around to go, this is for your trouble, and have a happy new year."

The man's eyes lit up as he looked at the money and said, "Yes, sir! No problem, and a happy new year to you!"

"That was a lot of money you gave him," Mary said.

"Mom, money is worthless after this life anyway," Pete said.

Jack laughed. "That's easy to say when it's not your hundred-dollar bill."

"I'll explain later," Pete replied. "Now, let's get out of here."

Shortly after eight, the five of them joined Steve and Margaret at the hotel, where, together, they were able to welcome in a joyous new year. Everyone agreed it was beautiful to sing "Auld Lang Syne" together.

Chapter Thirty-Five

The next day was Tuesday, January 1, 1991. Pete and Pam slept in but were awakened by the phone ringing at nine-thirty. Pete's assistant manager Bill Jefferies was on the phone.

"Pete, this is Bill, and I have to apologize. Before I went on vacation, you instructed me to place another two hundred and fifty million dollars with Pan-American. I wrote it down but just remembered that I had to do it before I left. I'm sorry I'm so absent-minded. I promise to do it tomorrow when the market opens."

"No, don't you dare. Haven't you heard? Pan-American is worthless. You earned yourself a raise," Peter said excitedly.

"Wow!" his employee said. "I've been skiing in Colorado. I haven't heard a thing."

"You did well, Bill. I'll explain everything later. Enjoy the holiday, and I'll see you at work tomorrow."

As he hung up the phone, Pete said to his wife, "Maybe everything won't be so bad after all. Whatever happens, we can face it together. I've learned that as long as someone is alive, they have the ability to accomplish something. Once they pass on, they can do nothing."

"Honey," Pam said, "yesterday, you said your father appeared and talked you out of doing something terrible. I think other people will find that hard to believe."

"I don't care, Pam. It happened, or I would not be here today. He showed me the terrible effects my death would have on our grandchildren and how unhappy you would be if I died while you were still mourning the death of little Jerry." He put his arms around his wife and held her as he added, "He looked younger than I am, but it was Dad. I no longer doubt his account of the angel who saved him forty-five years ago."

The two separated after several seconds, and she said, "Just the same, honey, let's keep the event between us, as many people will not believe you."

The next day, Pete met with the press to provide transparency to the public on the situation. The immediate loss to the Central New York State thrift was smaller than initially expected, just under a half billion dollars. In addition, government auditors now expected Pan-American investors to recover twenty-three cents on the dollar. Also, the Resolution Trust Corporation still had assets to help the thrift make up the deficit.

Pete explained the details. He finished with, "The final amount needed to bring the thrift back into complete solvency is over ninety million dollars, and we are negotiating for loans in that amount. No layoffs are planned, and we will remain open for business. Finally, I was responsible for investing with Pan-American. As such, I stand ready to offer my resignation as general manager of the Central New York Savings and Loan Association."

"Mr. Bailey!" a reporter yelled. Then, after being recognized by Pete, he asked, "Isn't it true that others complained to the federal regulators that Ryan Campbell's hedge fund might be a fraud, and those complaints were ignored?"

"It's my understanding that such was the case," Pete replied.

"Then why would you feel the need to resign?" The reporter questioned.

"If there were others who had reservations, then I feel I should have looked closer. Our depositors' money is a sacred trust," was Pete's explanation.

After a few more questions, Oscar Brenner, the chairman of the thrift's board, stepped forward and asked to be heard. After permission was granted, He announced, "The board has met earlier, and we voted unanimously to retain Pete Bailey as our General Manager." They all shook hands with Pete.

As the meeting ended, the reporters all hurried to report their stories, either on air or in print, as the case may be. Among the news they released were the names of the three corporations that agreed to loan the money the savings and loan needed to remain in operation. They were Wainwright Industries, owned by the family of George's deceased childhood friend, Sam Wainwright; Curtis Industries (owned by Jack and Carole Curtis); and an investment group headquartered in the United Kingdom. The chairman of that organization had been befriended by George Bailey during a trip to New York years ago.

The loans were all paid off by the year 2005, when Pete retired at the age of 72. However, Pete always maintained the happiest day of his life was the New Year's Eve celebration back in 1990, when he and his wonderful friends toasted the New Year with the knowledge that where there is life, there is always hope.

About the Author

Neil Mitchell was born in Mississippi to a farming family. His father was a Navy veteran of the Second World War who returned to his previous occupation after peace was established.

After two crop failures, Neil's father joined the U. S. Air Force, which gave Neil the opportunity to travel extensively through the U. S. and Europe.

Following graduation from high school in Florida, Neil heeded Horace Greeley's admonition to go west. After receiving degrees in political science and accounting, he served three and a half years in the U. S. Army, becoming a first lieutenant in the Military Police corps, where he served as military police operations officer and company executive officer. After discharge from the military, he pursued dual occupations as a teamster—eventually becoming shop steward—and a tax preparer, in which role he received the Earned Agent designation from the IRS.

Neil retired from transportation and delivery work in 2012. Now, in addition to maintaining a tax practice, he spends his time writing. This is his sixth published work, with more stories in the planning stage.

Neil, a widower with two living children, fourteen grandchildren, and six great-grandchildren, makes his home in Provo, Utah.